THE SHOTLEY INCIDENT

Alan Peck

ALAN PECK PUBLISHING

THE SHOTLEY INCIDENT
Copyright © Alan Peck , 2007

All Rights Reserved

ISBN 978-0-9550006-1-1

First Published 2007 by
Alan Peck Publishing
alanpeckpublishing@hotmail.co.uk

This novel is a work of fiction. Names, characters and incidents are either the product of the author's imagination or are used fictitiously. Any resemblance to actual persons, either living or dead, or events is entirely coincidental.

Printed in the UK by PrintonDemand-worldwide.com
Edited by Cambridge Editorial Partnership Ltd.

THE SHOTLEY INCIDENT

To Olive
My sounding board, proofreader, caterer and loving wife.

CHAPTER 1

It was a bad place to find a dead body. He shouldn't have been there: the signs clearly stated 'DANGER – KEEP OUT – TRESPASSERS WILL BE PROSECUTED'.

Simon Lake was only there to reminisce; the last time he'd been there was forty-four years ago to the day. On that day he had joined some two hundred other young lads at Ipswich station. Full of trepidation they had boarded buses to make the twelve-mile journey out to HMS Ganges at Shotley – their home for the next year.

On a bitterly cold January day, in nearly a foot of snow, he had said goodbye to his parents and to what he would soon realise had been a very comfortable life as a Suffolk schoolboy. He knew it would be very different but, like all the boys on that bus, he had never imagined quite how different it would be and quite what a rude shock awaited them.

Ganges was a forbidding Royal Navy training establishment in the village of Shotley Gate, situated on a peninsula that bisected the rivers Orwell and Stour. It afforded a commanding view over grey water to the ports of Felixstowe and Harwich. The place was a veritable monument to discipline and old-fashioned standards. Its aim was to take pampered scruffy schoolboys and turn them into real men, and it had achieved exactly that with the many thousands of boys who had passed through its grim gates over the years.

Sitting next to Simon on the bus that day was Dave Chandler, a big Scouse lad he could barely understand, but who seemed to Simon to be as hard as nails. He had long fair hair flowing down over the collar of his black leather jacket. Simon stared admiringly at Dave's tight blue denim jeans and black winkle-picker shoes. Dave talked loudly of the many scrapes he had been in and of the fights he had won, both in and out of the boxing ring,

Simon felt the anxiety growing within him. He had never come across anyone quite as hard as Dave and he felt that if all the boys were anything like him then he would struggle to survive in this alien new world.

After they alighted from the bus on to the stark, snow-covered parade ground they were allocated to their mess. This was an austere green hut constructed from wood and corrugated iron, which appeared to have no heating at all.

The Petty Officer Instructor smiled as he heard one lad remark that it was as cold in the hut as it was outside. He barked at them that with forty boys living together in such a small space they had no need to worry, as it would be adequately heated by their sweaty bodies. As Simon stood there shivering and forlorn this seemed difficult to believe.

He was relieved to see that Dave had been allocated to the same mess. Although he was in awe of him he was the only boy he had spoken to, so at least he knew there was somebody he could talk to.

They were ordered to strip and to put a towel around their waist and plimsolls on their feet, in readiness for a shower. The shower block was on the opposite side of the parade ground and they realised with utter disbelief that they were expected to wade through the deep snow to reach it.

The next shock came when they arrived at the shower block and discovered that there was no hot water. The instructor had no pity and yelled at them to get their towels off. As they cowered under the freezing torrent of water every boy knew that he was entering a very different environment from anything he had ever experienced before.

Each boy was allocated an iron bed and a grey steel locker in their spartan new home. The floor was polished wood – in fact it was so highly polished it was like a mirror. The walls were painted grey and the hut was completely devoid of any home comforts. Simon thought briefly of his bedroom at home, a warm and cosy haven – he wondered why on earth he had ever wanted to leave it.

Just inside the entrance to the mess was the cleanest dustbin he had ever seen. It shone spectacularly under the bare electric light bulbs and he couldn't imagine that anyone had ever dared to put any rubbish in it.

On the walls, precisely positioned and equally spaced out, were ten framed pictures of warships. Simon stared at them in awe and wondered if the day would ever come when he would escape from this awful place and actually serve on board a real ship. Finally, at the end of the most nerve-shredding day Simon had ever lived through, they were ordered in to bed and the lights went out.

As he tried to reflect on a day that seemed like a very bad dream, he heard a muffled noise from the next bed, just three feet away. With a shock he realised it was Dave – he was crying his eyes out under the blankets. Never again was he to see the brash, cocky Dave that he had met on the bus. In a strange sort of way Simon had been comforted by this.

During that long cold night he heard boys sobbing all around him. Some of them were just mumbling under the covers but some were audibly asking for their Mum. He did at least salvage a tiny semblance of self-esteem by somehow managing to keep back the tears.

Eventually the exhausted Simon drifted into a very troubled sleep, which was abruptly and terrifyingly ended at six o'clock in the morning. An immaculate-looking Petty Officer, who looked as if he'd been up for hours, was repeatedly crashing the lid of the dustbin up and down. He was screaming at the top of his very loud voice that he wanted to see all their feet on the deck instantly. Boys were stumbling out of bed with a mixture of fatigue and fear on their faces.

Later that day, after they had all been incessantly shouted at, issued with their uniforms and given brutally short haircuts, their humbling was complete. They all knew that they were now the lowest form of life in the entire universe.

In retrospect, this mutual loss of status had initiated the beginnings of some sort of bonding process. Simon really didn't fear Dave any more – they both knew they were at the very bottom of the food chain. He was surprised and maybe just a little proud that he seemed to be handling things a bit better than Dave was. There was no point in bravado any more – they knew they had to focus all their energy on to just getting through each day.

Since that time, Simon had often mused that it was doubtful if any boy who passed through Ganges could honestly say that he had enjoyed it. However, in later years nearly all of them considered it to be the most character-building episode in their entire life. He had never met anyone who didn't consider that they left Ganges a far more disciplined and well-rounded individual. It was a year of hell, which had instilled in Simon such qualities as respect, pride, smartness and punctuality. He felt it had given him a fundamental understanding of right and wrong and established a framework within which he would live the rest of his life.

Outsiders often claimed that Ganges boys were brutally bullied into subservience, but Simon had never taken that view. His instructors had been as hard as nails but absolutely fair. He had frequently been shouted at but had never once been sworn at or had a finger laid on him. In fact, while he was at Ganges he had never once seen any person in authority lay a finger on any boy, other than to show how sloppily they were dressed, how pathetically they marched or how lazily they saluted.

He left Ganges with a feeling of utter relief but also with a sense of gratitude that he had been turned into a far better person and that life was unlikely to ever be as tough again.

He remembered the one defining moment when he knew they were nearly at the end and that they had made it. Their Instructor, Petty Officer Ron Harris, had been marching them down the hill to the waterfront for their final boat drill when one of his fellow Instructors was walking past in the opposite direction. The other Instructor had grinned and shouted out: "They look like a right rabble, Ron".
To their delight he replied simply, "They'll do".
It was the ultimate accolade from PO Harris. It was as if he had told them he loved them and all the boys felt the pleasure of acceptance surge through them.

Simon often wondered what had happened to all those boys. After leaving Ganges most of them went off in different directions and he only ever saw a handful of them again. He wondered what they all did now, where they lived, who they had married and how many of them had died.

He often marvelled that upon leaving the Navy after nine years service he had been able to go to university and then ultimately qualify as a chartered accountant.

Simon was now a happily married man with two lovely children and a beautiful home. He was a partner in a well-established accountancy firm in Ipswich and he had acquired all the trappings of success that went with such a position.

When he left home on that cold Sunday morning it was to enjoy a few quiet hours on his own. His wife Pippa was away for the weekend, visiting an old friend in Norfolk. Simon was at a loose end but when he opened the Sunday Telegraph and saw the date, 8th January, he knew that it was a significant day.

He had been to Shotley many times to walk along the waterfront and peer through the iron railings at the haunting remains of Ganges. The Navy had vacated it back in the seventies and although part of it had briefly been used as a police training centre, it had now fallen in to decay.

Some of the buildings had been demolished but he could still see the old drill shed, the guardhouse, some of the mess accommodation and the monolithic central messing galley, where two thousand boys had eaten their every meal. The most iconic reminder of times past that was still standing was the famous old mast, which every boy had to climb.

Another poignant reminder was 'Faith, Hope and Charity' – three flights of steep steps leading down to the waterfront that would never be forgotten by any Ganges boy. When returning from boating on the river the instructors used the steps to let a class know how well or how badly they had done.

If they had carried out the boat drill correctly, scrubbed the boat until it was spotless and generally behaved perfectly, they only made one trip back up those steps. If the instructor was in any way displeased with them for any reason they would be sent up and down until they'd paid the price. On each journey up the steps the boys prayed that the torture would soon end. Every time the instructor shouted 'down again' their spirits would sink: hearts pounding, lungs working overtime, legs feeling like lead.

His plan that day had been to simply go for a walk and then to have lunch in the King's Head pub, which was situated on the periphery of the Ganges site, overlooking the waterfront. There were numerous gaps in the railings bordering the grounds and to Simon it had always been a temptation to ignore the warning signs and squeeze through for a closer look at whatever remained.

Glancing at his watch he realised he was far too early for lunch and so he decided to chance it. He couldn't see any security guard and there were very few people around. He figured that even if he was challenged he could simply explain that he was an ex-Ganges boy, simply there to relive some old memories.

He walked unsteadily over rough ground strewn with rubble and realised that he was crossing the remains of what had once been 'The Long Covered Way'. This was an array of brick-built messes spanning either side of a long covered concrete walkway that stretched all the way from the Quarterdeck down nearly to the shoreline.

After an initial month in the annexe for new entrants Simon had moved into one of these, namely Blake 7 Mess. This had been his home for the rest of his time there and he was sad to see that it had been bulldozed flat. He wondered sadly why people couldn't just leave things as they were if they weren't going to actually redevelop the place.

He decided to walk on and find the remains of the area the Navy had dubbed The Quarterdeck – a large open rectangular area that boys could only cross at the double. Being caught walking here had always been a sure way to incur the wrath of one of the many eagle-eyed Instructors. Simon figured it would feel good now just to stroll across it with hands in pockets and break those old rules.

It was then that he saw the body – face down, with one leg straight and the other bent at the knee. The head was face down and the arms were out at the sides, as if in position to attempt a press-up. The hair was blonde and long, and he knew immediately that the body was that of a young female. She was dressed in a black bomber jacket, blue jeans and trainers. Acting as if on auto-pilot, he bent down to look at the face. He touched her cheek and with a start he thought he could detect some faint warmth. He felt a combination of hope and panic course through him.

Without thinking he got on his knees, rolled the body over and attempted both heart massage and the kiss of life. He was shocked now at how cold her face was against his and when he could find no sign of breathing he felt both her neck and her wrist, desperately hoping to locate a pulse.

He quickly realised there was absolutely no hope and wondered if he'd been wrong in ever thinking there had been any detectable body heat. Panic was rising within him and as it overcame the initial numbness of shock he began to wonder if he had been wrong to even touch her. By now there would be masses of evidence of his presence for the forensics people to find. He had to contact the police, and fast.

His hands shook uncontrollably as he fumbled inside his coat pocket for the mobile. A whirlwind of thoughts raced through his head – what was she doing here? He gave no thought to how she might have died – he just knew from his instincts that it was murder. How would he explain what he was doing here?

Eventually he steadied his trembling hands sufficiently to dial 999 and then he waited in trepidation for the sound of approaching sirens. He stared at her face – pretty, even features, almost delicate, but too much make-up. The red lipstick was smeared and he involuntarily drew the back of his hand across his mouth. Surprisingly her hands were quite rough – she looked too young and feminine to do manual work.

He didn't know how long they took to arrive but when he heard the first siren he rushed round to the old main gate. He saw a police Volvo estate stopped on the far side with blue light flashing and two burly PCs clambering over the barbed wire topped gates.

A panicky Simon blurted out "quick, this way" and started to run. The PCs were right behind him; voices on their walkie-talkies were asking for details of their location. More sirens heralded the arrival of reinforcements and as he arrived back at the body Simon struggled to control the words tumbling from his mouth: "I was out for a walk and I just stumbled across her."

The PCs were quiet, ignoring the hubbub of noise and checking for signs of breathing.
        "I thought she was warm – I tried massage and the kiss of life. I couldn't just leave her … not if there was any chance … I had to touch her."

The older of the two PCs clambered to his feet.
        "Okay, sir, please stand well clear, keep still and just don't touch anything else. We're going to have to preserve the scene and get more help out here. Then we'll start taking details from you."

The PC pressed a button on the walkie-talkie and told whoever was at the other end that a body, female, had been located on the old Ganges site and that they urgently needed backup, a doctor and forensics.

More police arrived and soon there was a ring of yellow-jacketed officers using reels of tape to cordon off a wide area all around the body. An Inspector took charge, a doctor examined the body and eventually Simon was led away to one of the police cars. He was glad of the warmth and realised just how cold he had become.

The Inspector asked Simon how he had travelled there and then enquired politely if he felt able to drive his own car and follow them back to the station. They drove him down to the waterfront to collect his car and then one of the officers travelled with him in the passenger seat as they followed the police car back towards Ipswich. It was a couple of miles before Simon realised that there was another police car behind them. He wondered if all these policemen really needed to head back to base or if they were actively taking no chances with him.

On arrival at the police station Simon was taken to an interview room and given a much-needed mug of hot sweet tea. The senior policeman who had attended the murder scene arrived and he now introduced himself as Detective Inspector Alan Whitley. He also introduced PC Stephen Golding and explained that they would be taking a full statement, which would be recorded and then word-processed for Simon to check and sign. They sat on one side of a bare wooden desk and Simon on the other. Apart from a filing cabinet there was nothing else in the room.

Simon was shocked when the DI asked if he would like legal representation present whilst making the statement. Simon thought he was simply a witness, albeit a very key witness, but he was starting to feel like a suspect. He decided that he was simply going to give a totally factual and honest account of everything and that there couldn't be any risk in this. He resolved that if they started asking any follow-up questions he would then ask for the company's solicitor, John Black, to be present before going any further.

Simon was edgy and far from his usual lucid self. He was shocked at making the discovery but also awkward and defensive about just what he was doing trespassing on private property. He knew he wasn't coming across well but DI Whitley was sympathetic and understanding, telling him to take a few deep breaths and not to hurry.

Simon decided to start right at the beginning by explaining about his time at Ganges and that today was the anniversary of his joining the Royal Navy all those years ago. This was all provable via MoD records and he felt a little easier once he realised this. He then explained his exact movements that morning in great detail.

When he had finished his account the DI explained that he would have it typed and printed out right away and that he would like Simon to remain at the station for the time being. Simon agreed and stated that in the meantime he would make some calls from his mobile.

The PC went to get him another mug of tea and Simon made the first call to Pippa, who he knew would be lunching with Glenda, an old school friend who now lived at Holt in Norfolk. Glenda answered and put Pippa on the line. "Hi darling, how are you managing without me?"
He paused. "Well I'm okay but I've had a bit of a traumatic morning, not what I'd planned at all."
There was silence from the other end.
          "I went for a walk and found a dead body. I'm at the police station now – I've just been making a statement."

There was a sharp intake of breath from Pippa. "Bloody hell, what body, where?"

"On the old Ganges site, I decided to go for a walk to see what was left of it and I came across a girl's body."
Another gasp. "A girl? Who was she?"

"I don't know. I don't think the police know yet."

"Was there anyone else around?"

"No, not a soul."

"Bloody hell, how terrible. I didn't even know you could walk there – I thought it was all sealed off with Keep Out signs."
Simon paused. "Well, it is, but there are lots of gaps in the fence."

"Jesus, Simon, so you were trespassing when you found her body?"

"Well yes, but it's no big deal. Local people walk their dogs there. I don't think anyone much cares about walkers nosing around so long as they don't steal anything. The owners of the site would have a problem with builders turning up and pinching stuff but I can't see that they'd care much about Ganges old boys just having a look around the place for old time's sake."

Pippa was shocked to say the least. She had no idea of Simon's plans for the day and had assumed that he would either have a sandwich for lunch or that he would walk to the local pub. To learn that he had stumbled across a dead girl's body on the old Ganges site was hard to take in. He did his best to calm her down but it was difficult as he felt so edgy himself.

"Look Simon, I'm going to head for home right now."

"There's no point, darling. You might as well stay there for lunch and come home later. I'm going to be at the police station for a while yet."

"Have you contacted a solicitor?"
She was ever pragmatic and Simon knew that she already feared that he might get himself into deep water.

"That's going to be my next call. I'm going to ask John Black to come over here."

"Good idea. I'll just have a quick bite to eat and then I'm coming home. If you aren't there when I arrive I'll call the station. I need to see you, Simon – you've had one hell of a shock and I'm worried about you."

"Okay darling, but please don't get yourself in to a state. I'm okay and I just want to help the police all I can."

CHAPTER 2

When Simon called John Black he struck lucky. He had been about to leave home for lunch at his golf club but readily agreed to come straight to the station. He was a jack-of-all-trades solicitor who had handled just about all the legal work for Chambers, Lake & Bradwell for as long as Simon could remember. Simon had also had all his personal legal work on things like house conveyancing and will-making done through Black's practice in Ipswich.

As soon as Black arrived at the station he sat Simon down and got him to talk through all of the events of the day, particularly the details of precisely what had happened once the police had arrived on the scene. He was concerned that Simon hadn't called him earlier but once he had a chance to go through the statement he seemed satisfied that Simon hadn't said anything to incriminate himself.

Black sat opposite Simon and stared straight in to his eyes. "Look, Simon, they don't yet know how the girl died. If they were to establish that she was murdered then you need to understand that the police will have to consider you a suspect. It is standard practice in any murder investigation. The person finding the body has to be eliminated from suspicion, no matter what the circumstances."

Simon already knew as much – he'd watched enough television to know the drill. What worried him was just how they would eliminate him. He had touched the girl's body, attempted to resuscitate her, placed his mouth over hers – and there were no other witnesses. He had a genuine reason for being there and he had absolutely no motive for killing anyone, but how could he prove that?

He wondered what on earth an attractive young girl would be doing there on a cold Sunday morning – had she been walking a dog and then been attacked by a would-be rapist?

They chewed over the possibilities for a while and then DI Whitley entered the room and took the seat on the opposite side of the table from Simon and John Black.

"The doctor has confirmed that the girl is dead and he has carried out a preliminary investigation. There are marks on her neck that would be consistent with strangulation but that is just speculation at this stage. It doesn't appear that her clothing has been interfered with and a purse containing cash, credit cards and a driving licence was found in her jacket pocket."

While Simon sat there stunned by the news, Black was quick to interject, "So, who was she?"

"I can't tell you that until we've notified her next of kin and had a positive identification, but the name on all the documentation is consistent and the photo on the driving licence certainly looks like her. I can tell you that the driving licence is that of a 22-year-old female with an Ipswich address. We have also located her car. "

Simon looked up. "Where was it?"

DI Whitley looked into Simon's face intently. "On the waterfront, by the pub – almost next to where you were parked, actually."

Simon gasped and sat back, arms outstretched, gripping the table and trying to keep composed. "Well there aren't many parking spaces on the front, so I guess that's not unusual."

Whitley continued watching Simon's face carefully. "No, I guess not."

Black interjected. "So, can my client go home now?"

Whitley looked at Simon, "Yes, but I have to ask you to notify us of your whereabouts as we may need to contact you urgently depending on how our enquiries progress. Also you need to be aware that the press will be hounding you and I strongly advise you to make absolutely no comment to them whatsoever."

Whitley turned to look at John Black, "I think your solicitor will endorse this advice."

Black nodded vigorously, "Absolutely right – if you give them anything at all then quite apart from the possibility of hindering the judicial process they won't give you or Pippa a minute's peace. You need to really let them know that 'No Comment' means exactly that and will continue to mean exactly that."

Simon nodded – he'd already resolved not to talk to the media anyway. He gave Whitley his home, office and mobile numbers, explaining that he expected to be in the Ipswich area all week doing routine work for clients.

As he headed for home he wondered quite how he was going to have a routine week at work. In his heart he knew he would be spending much of his time talking to the police as more details came to light.

He told himself that all he had done was to stumble accidentally upon a dead body – he had attempted resuscitation, he hadn't committed any crime, he had stayed with the body and had immediately contacted the police. He couldn't have done any more. Okay, so technically he shouldn't have been there but nobody was going to worry about that. Maybe he shouldn't have touched the body but he felt that anyone in his situation, believing there was any tiny chance of revival, should at least attempt it. What if a post-mortem had revealed that she was probably in the last throes of life when he'd found her and that she could possibly have been saved if he'd only taken the right action?

Simon wondered again what on earth she was doing there. There had been maybe four or five cars parked on the waterfront but the only people he'd seen were a couple of dog walkers headed along the waterfront and away from the Ganges site. Girls of her age were usually tucked up in bed having a lie-in on a cold Sunday morning. It was usually lunchtime before anyone much arrived there for a drink or a meal in the pub, followed by a walk along the front to look at the yachts in the marina and to gaze across the water to the massive container ships in Felixstowe docks.

He wished he'd asked Whitley whether they'd found any sign of a loose dog in the area. No doubt the police were already pursuing this and many other angles too. Not only was it a strange place to find a body, but it was such a strange time, unless he'd been totally wrong about sensing some body warmth and she'd actually been there all night.

As soon as he pulled into the driveway Pippa ran out of the house and hugged him. He wrapped his arms around her and then held her at arm's length – she had tears in her eyes and her face was ghostly white. He led her inside and they sat down on either side of the table in the dinette.

He attempted a smile of reassurance. "It's okay, darling; a horrible experience but nothing to panic about."
She certainly wasn't convinced. "What is happening? Do they know who she is yet?"
He nodded. "It seems so, but they wouldn't tell me or John. A 22-year-old Ipswich girl was all they would say. They found her driving licence and credit cards in her purse."
"Had she been raped?"
"I don't think so; her clothing didn't seem to have been disturbed at all. The police doctor apparently said it was too soon to give a cause of death but there were marks on her neck that would be consistent with strangulation."
Pippa gasped. "Oh my God, how awful. How terrible for her family. Did she have a wedding ring on?"

"No idea – I didn't even think to look. I was in such a panic. I tried heart massage and giving her the kiss of life but it was all too late."

"So you touched her?"

"I had to. She was face down but I thought her body was still warm – I turned her over."

Pippa's face was ashen. "Should you have done that?"

Simon reacted angrily. "Well what the hell was I supposed to do? Just let her die? The one thing I've always remembered from all that first aid training in the Navy was resuscitation techniques. I'd always thought that one day I might need it but … it was too late anyway. But it was the right thing to do – we always had it drilled into us that you made every effort you possibly could until you were one hundred per cent certain that there was absolutely no hope whatsoever of revival. You're not supposed to stand around wondering about the preservation of evidence; you're supposed to try any damned thing you can to save someone's life. "

She was chastened. "I'm sorry but I'm just worried about how the police would view all this."

"With an open mind, I hope. So what do you think I should have done – turned and run?"

She shook her head. "No, of course not. It's just a bloody shame you ever went there at all, you just can't seem to let your old Navy days rest."

Simon bridled. "Well, thanks for all your support and understanding. What a terrible crime it is to risk going for a walk where local people already walk their dogs every day of the week. I'm so sorry your cosy little life has been inconvenienced by this girl."

Pippa burst into tears and rose from the chair, moving around the table towards him. He looked away, shrugged her off and stormed upstairs to his study, closing the door behind him.

Simon loved his study. This was his refuge – he did much of his accountancy work here but it was also his bolthole when he wanted to be on his own – modern man's equivalent of the shed.

CHAPTER 3

Simon switched on the radio to hear the local news, and it was no surprise that they already knew the bare bones of this breaking story. It was the main item, which was also no surprise. Following the multiple murders of prostitutes in the Ipswich area in 2006 there was bound to be huge interest in the finding of a young female body.

They had nothing that Simon didn't already know, just giving the basic details and saying that the body had yet to be positively identified.

Surprisingly it was nearly nine o'clock that evening before the phone rang.

"Hello, Mr. Lake, it's DI Whitley here."

"Oh, hello. Any more news?"

"Yes, the body has now been formally identified as Kelly Taylor, a 22-year-old florist living and working in Ipswich. Does the name mean anything to you?"

"No, not a thing. Did she work in a florist shop?"

"Yes, in 'Flowers For You' in the town centre."

"I know it, near the Corn Exchange."

"Yes, that's right. Have you ever been in there?"

"No, I get most flowers for my wife at Tesco or on special occasions at 'Anglian Blooms' on Fore Street. Have you confirmed the cause of death yet?"

"Officially no, but off the record it was almost certainly compression to the neck, strangulation to you and I."

Simon took a deep breath. "So it's a murder investigation?"

"Yes, it looks that way. I'd like to ask you to come in to the station first thing in the morning, say eight o'clock. Is that okay?"

"Yes, sure. I've got a busy week mapped out in my diary, but when you find a dead body then I understand the need to prioritise stuff."

"Thank you, I hope we won't need to call you during the night and I appreciate your cooperation."

Simon replaced the receiver and stared out of the window. A florist; that would explain the rough hands. He knew that floristry wasn't the delicate profession many people imagined it to be. He'd seen them in the back of the shop stripping thorns and leaves from roses, with their hands in and out of cold water all the time.

A contrite Pippa brought him in a mug of coffee; he always liked one around this time. He didn't have problems getting to sleep at night ... usually.

"I heard the phone go. Who was it?"

"The police. They've identified the body. They want me to go in to the station first thing in the morning."

"Who was she?"

"A florist by the name of Kelly Taylor. She worked in 'Flowers For You'."

"I know it. I used them not long ago to send flowers by relay order to Aunt Beth on her birthday."

"Did you notice a girl with long blonde hair?"

"No, it was Jayne, the boss lady, who served me."

"Well, I'd better call Peter and tell him what's happened and that I'll be late in tomorrow. He'll need to explain things to Charles Dalton as I was going to spend most of the week on his year-end stuff."

Peter Chambers was the founder of the firm and the senior partner in Chambers, Lake & Bradwell. Simon went to work for him as a newly qualified CA some thirty years ago and had been a partner for some ten years now. The firm had grown consistently, with a varied client base of small to medium local businesses and farmers. The staff had risen to over thirty people and they were housed in comfortable red-brick offices near the town centre.

Peter was shocked by the news but promised to let everyone in the office know what had happened and also to let them know that they would have to cover Simon's absence as best they could. Peter would also personally call Simon's main client and assure him that Simon would be back on his case just as soon as he returned from the police station.

Simon also called Chris Bradwell, the third and youngest partner in the firm. Having previously worked as an accountant in the IT sector, Chris had been responsible for overseeing the installation of an impressive local area network, which brought the business well and truly in to the twenty-first century. He had also personally installed high-specification PCs and broadband links in both Peter's and Simon's houses, which enabled them both to work from home. He suggested that Simon might find it easier to work mostly from home until things settled down, and he offered to transport any files or equipment that he might need.

His largest client, and the person likely to be most inconvenienced by events, was Charles Dalton. A local property magnate and entrepreneur who owned offices, shops and houses all over Ipswich and the surrounding areas, Charles was right out of the top drawer - an old Etonian, councillor and Rotarian. He was a long-standing client and Chambers, Lake & Bradwell owed much of their success to his ever-growing empire. Simon was supposed to be overseeing the preparation of Charles' year-end accounts and, as ever, Charles was insistent that Simon should not miss a trick in the quest to reduce his tax liability to the absolute minimum.

It was a night of fitful sleep, full of dreams that were all too realistic. He was up by six, listening to the radio as he shaved and showered. They didn't have any fresh news and said nothing of the girl's name or work. He made coffee and turned on the TV in the kitchen/diner, switching to BBC News 24. They were running it as one of the lead stories – partly because of the very remote possibility that it could somehow be linked to the multiple prostitute murders.

Pippa joined him. She was far from her usual immaculate self, looking as if she'd had even less sleep than he had.

"It'll be a long day, darling; let me make you a proper breakfast."
He shook his head. "No thanks, just cereal and a slice of toast – I couldn't stomach anything more."

"Will you call me when you're finished at the station? Once you get to work you'll never get a chance."

"Okay, don't worry. I don't know what time I'll be home. I think I'll just have to play today by ear."

He kissed her and backed his car out of the garage. Despite the usual early build-up of commuter traffic, he was at the police station in ten minutes. The place was a hive of activity and after he finally found a parking space he had to skirt around a group of news reporters.

A hassled-looking DI Whitley met him just inside the main entrance and led Simon straight to an interview room.

"First things first, Mr. Lake – have you come by car?"
"Yes."

"Is it the car you went to Shotley in yesterday?"

"Yes, it's the only one I've got."

"Well, I have to ask you for the keys, please. Forensics need to check it over."
Alarm bells rang in Simon's head. "What for?"

"Just standard practice, I'm afraid. You will also need to undergo a DNA test."

"Well, traces of my DNA must be all over the girl's body but you won't find anything in my car."

"Don't worry, Mr. Lake – we just have to check everything. It really is just standard practice – we need to be able to eliminate you."

"Could there be traces of the girl's DNA that have been transferred from her body on to mine and then in to my car? I don't know how DNA works …"

"Please don't worry, Mr. Lake. At this stage we just have to collect all the evidence we possibly can."

The rest of the morning was spent going over the previous day's events in minute detail, again and again. Simon struggled with the timings of just when he had left home, when he parked at Shotley and how long he'd been out of the car before he found the body.

He hadn't taken much notice of time because he'd had all of Sunday to simply please himself – it wasn't like a working day with appointments and all sorts of time-specific events happening. The only time he could remember looking at his watch was when he had decided it was too early for lunch – that must have been around eleven.

Whitley asked him again for exact details of which cars were parked on the waterfront when he arrived. Simon couldn't really remember anything other than that there were a few cars there, perhaps four or five.

Whitley looked at him intently. "Did you notice a silver BMW 3 series coupe with an 06 plate?"
Simon thought long and hard. "No, sorry – I really didn't give any thought to any of the cars there. Why?"

"Because that was Kelly Taylor's car."

"Wow, that's a flash car for a young florist."

"Yes, that's exactly what I thought."

"I've been racking my brains to try to figure out what on earth she was doing there on a cold Sunday morning. Could she have been walking a dog?"

"Apparently not; we asked her parents about that and nobody in the family has a dog."

"Don't her family know why she was there?"

"No, it seems that Kelly was a very independent girl with lots of friends, always coming and going. No steady boyfriend that they knew of, but she was never short of admirers. Her mum and dad could never keep tabs on where she was or what she was doing."

"I wonder where the money for a smart car came from? Are her parents well off?"

"No, they live in a terraced council house. Clean and tidy, nice people, but definitely no sign of affluence."

"They must be devastated."

"They are. It's the worst thing we ever have to do – breaking that sort of news to parents."

Simon braced himself to ask the next question. "Do you have any idea of the time of death?"

"Well, we'll have to wait for the findings of the post-mortem, but the doctor is of the opinion that she hadn't been dead for long when you raised the alarm."

"So what happens now?"

"We've erected a tent at the scene and the forensics people will probably be working there all day. We have a team of policemen going door to door around the whole area to find out if anyone saw anything and we're putting out an appeal through the media. I'm hoping that a dog walker might have seen something."

"What about the landlord of the pub – did he or his wife see anything?"

"No, he was one of the first people we visited. It seems that they had a long lie-in after a really busy Saturday night. I was hoping he might have noticed what cars were outside on the front, but it seems he didn't even look out of the window until late morning."

It was lunchtime when Whitley asked Simon if he wanted a lift back to his home or to the office. He explained that they would need to keep his car until the forensic examination was complete. Simon decided he really didn't want anyone seeing him in a police car and opted to call Pippa and get her to collect him. She was at the station within ten minutes, looking flustered and worried.

Simon managed a weak smile. "Hello, darling, can you give me a lift to the office?"

She gripped his arm. "Oh, Simon, there are reporters and television people outside, and at the house. How do they know you are involved?"

"I guess it's impossible to keep it quiet for long. They're bound to be interested in whoever found the body."

"What can we do?"

"Just try to carry on as usual, as best we can. DI Whitley has advised me to make absolutely no comment to the media."

Whitley reappeared and introduced himself to Pippa. "Can I suggest that you both wait in a back room for a little while? We're going outside to tell the press that we'll be making a formal announcement in fifteen minutes' time. Once we've got them all in the conference room I suggest you two take the opportunity to leave in peace. Just let me know where you'll be if I need to contact you again later today."

Simon nodded. "I'll either be at the office or at home, but Pippa says the press are at our house. How do they know I found the body?"

Whitley shook his head. "I'm sorry, I honestly don't know – but they were bound to find out sooner or later. In the briefing I will tell them that you are cooperating fully but that you have no wish for any publicity. I'll ask them to respect that and most of them will, but there are always some who will pester anyone and everyone if they think they'll get even a word out of them. My advice is to keep saying 'No Comment' and absolutely nothing else. If you stick to that they'll soon give up, but if you say anything else then I can promise you they won't give you a minute's peace."

Simon had to ask the next question. "Will they think I'm a suspect?"

Whitley smiled sympathetically. "I'm afraid so – as I said before, anyone finding a dead body has to be eliminated from our enquiries."

Simon bristled. "But it's not very likely a killer would stay with the body and phone for the police, is it?"

Whitley smiled again. "No I suppose not … unless they did it to create an alibi."

Pippa gasped – Simon felt his whole body tense up.

Whitley showed them to an empty interview room and said they would be told when it was okay to leave. They both sat in stunned silence.

Pippa was shocked rigid by this sudden interruption to her comfortable life. Two years previously she had taken a very generous early retirement package to leave her job as the HR Manager for a large insurance company that had been merged with a rival.

She had taken up golf, got involved in charity work and enjoyed coffee mornings, shopping and pub lunches with her girl friends. The mortgage had long been paid off and Pippa had used part of her financial settlement to buy a little Mercedes SLK convertible. On a fine day she liked nothing more than putting the top down and heading for the golf club. She played in a regular foursome of girls who didn't take the game too seriously but who all loved the banter on the course and in the clubhouse over lunch.

Now she was sitting in a stark interview room looking at the troubled face of her husband, and she was determined to support him all she could.
She gripped his arm. "So where do you want to go?"

"To the office first. I need to let Peter know what's happening and then I'll take some work home with me. I don't want you going home alone if there are press there."

The door opened and a PC looked in. "The DI says the coast is clear. He suggests you leave now."
Looking nervously from side to side they walked quickly to the car and were at the office in minutes.

A relieved-looking Peter Chambers ushered them both straight in to his office. "What a terrible shock for you, Simon – and for you too, Pippa. We've had a number of calls from reporters but I've instructed everyone to reply 'No Comment'. I'm afraid everyone in the office knows that it was you that found the body – it was impossible to keep it under wraps."

"It's okay, Peter. Everyone seems to know anyway, or they soon will. Pippa says there are reporters at the house. I guess we're not going to get any peace for a while."
Peter smiled benignly. "Look, just take it a day at a time. If you want to take some time off then that's fine with me."
Simon shook his head. "No, I want to carry on as normally as possible. I might take some work home but I want to keep on top of everything. Does Charles Dalton know what's happened?"
Peter raised his eyebrows. "Yes, I called him earlier. He expressed his concern and hoped you would still be able to sort his year-end out ASAP – typical Charles."
Simon smiled. "If the end of the world was nigh Charles bloody Dalton would still want his pound of flesh. I'll take some of his

stuff home with me now and make a start on it. It might take my mind off everything else. My only problem is that the forensic people have got my car and we can't get more than a couple of shoeboxes into Pippa's."

"Well, if you need more of it moved just let us know and we'll get it to you. Can anyone else in the office help you out with it?"

"No, it's best I handle it. I've learned so much about the ins and outs of Dalton's wheeling and dealing over the years that it would be an absolute nightmare for anyone else to try to figure it all out."

When they arrived back at the house they had to negotiate around half a dozen reporters standing in the gateway leading in to their drive. It was a detached red-brick Georgian property in what was deemed to be the 'nice' part of Ipswich. As they got out of the car Pippa rushed into the house while Simon closed the gate and warded off the reporters with several "No comments".

They persisted with questions and Simon was dismayed to hear one of them shout, "Are you a suspect, Mr. Lake?"
He was relieved to shut the front door behind him and to see that Pippa was busy closing the lounge curtains. The phone was ringing incessantly, and when he could ignore it no longer he lifted the receiver and stuffed it under a cushion. They went into the kitchen and hugged each other tightly until Pippa held him at arm's length and asked if he would like some lunch. All he wanted was a sandwich and coffee.

They turned on the TV and watched the press briefing on the lunchtime news. The conference room was packed with reporters and cameramen all jostling for space. It was simple and factual and Whitley made it evident from the outset that no questions would be taken. This didn't stop them all trying once Whitley had finished reading his typed statement. He simply gathered up his papers, thanked everyone and briskly left the room.

CHAPTER 4

Simon spent the afternoon in his study working on Charles Dalton's accounts. There were umpteen parts to the Dalton empire and over twenty different bank accounts, several of which were offshore. Despite being a multi-millionaire who need never work again, Dalton was driven by the acquisition of wealth. Despite Simon using just about every measure of tax avoidance known to man, Dalton was always convinced he should be paying out less than he was.

He had always insisted on Simon doing most of his work even though he knew much of it could have been delegated to more junior and less expensive staff. Dalton took the view that having a partner do most of his work was a costly but necessary expense. He was dismissive toward the clerical staff in the office but he always wanted evidence of just how Simon was using every trick in the book to minimise his liability to the Inland Revenue.

There were occasional callers at the front door as the waiting reporters dreamed up excuses to try again. Pippa resorted to watching from a crack in the curtains and only answering the door to anyone she recognised. Through the afternoon the reporters gradually gave up and disappeared one by one. Simon had reluctantly decided that he would have to use the phone. The home number was ex-directory but still some unwanted calls came through. Each time he simply gave out "No comment" and put the receiver down.

By the end of the afternoon Simon knew that he needed a lot more stuff shipped across from the office if he was to carry on working at home. He preferred working in the office, but it was obvious that it would be awkward until things quietened down. There were boxes stacked in his office containing Dalton's bank statements, invoices, receipts and all manner of other paperwork.

He called Chris Bradwell, who was happy to help. Chris had a huge Volvo estate and he always kept the rear seats folded flat to maximise the load space. He promised to get one of the office juniors to load everything Simon wanted into his car and said he would drop everything off on his way home at the end of the day.

Simon and Pippa watched the early evening news in the kitchen/diner while they ate a microwaved shepherd's pie. The murder only warranted a thirty-second slot on the national news as there were big developments in Iraq and a high-profile politician defecting from the Labour party. It received detailed coverage on the local television news, though, with film footage of Ganges, Shotley Gate village, Kelly's home and the shop where she had worked.

The lady who owned the florist shop was interviewed and stated that Kelly Taylor had been a lovely bubbly girl, a good florist who was very popular with all of the staff and the customers. She wiped away the tears as she recalled the fun and laughter in the shop whenever Kelly was around.

Simon was immensely relieved that his name wasn't mentioned. They simply stated that "The body was found by an Ipswich man who'd been out for a walk".
The local radio stations and the evening paper were repeating this same message. Simon doubted that the tabloid hacks would be as circumspect, and warned Pippa to expect the worst once the following day's papers came off the press.

During the evening they made calls to their son Paul and daughter Chloe, who were both married and had moved away from the Ipswich area. Both were understandably shocked to hear the news and promised to do anything they possibly could to help.

DI Whitley called twice to check out minor details relating to Simon's statement, and Peter Chambers called to discuss some other work issues. Peter reiterated that he didn't want Simon to worry about work and assured him that, apart from Charles Dalton's year-end, everything else was being reallocated to others until things returned to normal.

Sleep didn't come easy as Simon and Pippa lay in bed talking through all that had happened. Apart from the obvious question of who did it, the biggest dilemma was why on earth Kelly would have been there at all. They also discussed how she could possibly have afforded to buy and run a nearly new BMW. Pippa speculated that maybe Kelly had arranged a secret meeting with somebody that had gone terribly wrong. Eventually, when they knew they weren't going to find any answers to the many questions, they drifted off in to a troubled sleep.

A hammering at the front door at just before seven, when it was still dark, rudely awakened them.
Pippa peered through a gap in the curtains and gasped. "Oh my God, it's the police."
He was out of bed and pulling on his dressing gown in seconds.
Whitley was at the door holding a piece of paper up in front of him. "I'm sorry, Mr. Lake, but we have a search warrant and we need to search the house."
Simon bristled. "What the hell for – and why now? Couldn't you have waited until we'd got up and had breakfast?"
Whitley looked down at his feet. "I am truly sorry but we have to do it now. I also have some officers at your place of work. We simply have to cover every angle in a murder enquiry. The sooner we make progress the sooner we can eliminate you and let you get on with life as normal."

Simon shook his head. "Okay, come in if you have to, but we'd appreciate it if you don't make a mess."

Pippa interjected, "And make bloody sure you all wipe your feet or I'll be giving you a cleaning bill."

Whitley smiled apologetically. "I really am very sorry, Mrs. Lake."

They went all over the house but it was clearly Simon's study that Whitley was most interested in. Simon stood in the doorway while Whitley and a PC went through the desk drawers and filing cabinets.

Eventually Whitley turned to face him. "Where do you keep the documentation for your car, Mr. Lake?"

Simon pulled open a suspended file drawer. "Some of it is at the office because it's a company car, but some of it is in here. And while we're on the subject of cars, when am I getting it back?"

Whitley took the file Simon handed to him. "Probably later today … or tomorrow at the latest. It takes time because the forensics people are very thorough – they have to be in their job."

Whitley glanced through the file and couldn't hide his satisfaction at finding a recent invoice for the last service. He glanced at it and looked up at Simon. "I'll need to borrow this for a while - I'll give you a signature for it."

Simon grunted. "No problem, I've got nothing to hide. I do think I deserve some explanation for all this though – I've been totally cooperative with you."

Whitley looked awkward. "We just need to check something out. I'll tell you all I can whenever we have any definite news. We will be making a press statement later this morning at which I'm going to confirm that the cause of death was strangulation."

Simon stared at him. "Do you know the time of death?"

"Well, after examination and … using the information that the doctor who attended the scene gave him, the pathologist puts it at between 1030 and 1130."

Simon was wide eyed. "Bloody hell, so I really did find her just after it happened?"

Whitley merely observed him, saying nothing.

"So I was right when I thought I detected some body heat?"

Whitley just looked at him.

It was late morning before they left, taking only one box full of Simon's personal papers with them. Peter had already phoned to say that they had searched Simon's office and asking if everything was okay.

"Yes, they've been here since seven going through the whole house. I hope they haven't made a mess of my office?"

"No, I was keeping an eye on them the whole time. They've taken a few files away though, mostly car stuff, but I've seen what they've taken and they've signed for it."

Simon took a deep breath. "What's the office gossip, then? Do they all think I did it?"

Peter attempted a chuckle. "I've told everybody that it's all just routine procedure whenever someone finds a body and it's an unexplained death. I said they simply need to eliminate you from their enquiries and then you'll be back at your desk. I've reassured them that you're busy at home working on Charles Dalton's year-end accounts."

"Well I've done sod all work this morning but I will try to when and if I ever get some peace and quiet."

"Just take your time and try not to get too stressed out. I'm sure it will all be sorted soon."

Pippa made them both coffee and they sat down to look at the coverage in the Telegraph. It was just factual reporting and Simon decided to get onto the computer – he was relieved they hadn't taken that away. He surfed the net for a while to see what the tabloids were saying but, apart from two of them naming the road, none of them had actually named him from what he could see.

He decided there was a good chance Whitley and his boys might come back for the computer, so he took a back-up of all the important stuff onto CD. He figured he could always get a replacement PC from the office if the worst came to the worst.

He spent the afternoon unenthusiastically doing a bit of work whilst taking occasional phone calls from friends and acquaintances. Some of them were from people genuinely worried and offering to do anything they could to help. Some were just people feigning concern and looking for some gossip from the inside. One was from Charles Dalton.

"Hello Simon, how are you, old man?"

"I'm okay, Charles, just wanting the police to catch whoever did it so I can resume normal life."

"I'm so sorry. Look … I've been thinking, you've got so much on your plate, why don't you let me find someone else to sort out my year-end?"

"No Charles, I wouldn't hear of it. Anyway there's no great rush, we don't have to file the accounts for ages yet. It will be a nightmare for anyone else to tackle and quite honestly I'm working on it right now, at home. I'm leaving everything else but Peter and I agreed that we can't let our best client down."

"Oh … I see. Right … well that's very good, but I want you to put yourself first until this all gets sorted out. I really don't mind if you want me to find someone else to do it so that you don't have to worry."

"No, really Charles – don't worry, it's no problem, I'll sort it."

He stared at the ceiling – sympathy and understanding from Charles Dalton – wonders would never cease! He stared around him at all the boxes full of Charles' paperwork – it was lucky that the boys in blue hadn't taken all of them away. That would have seriously tested Charles's patience.

CHAPTER 5

Pippa decided to cook Simon one of her special beef stews that night. They tried to lighten their mood with large gin and tonics followed by a good bottle of Merlot with the meal. Try as she might, though, Pippa couldn't cheer him up. He was totally preoccupied with his thoughts, wondering what the hell was going on. They'd had police crawling over the house and he was still without his car – Simon was starting to get really mad. Over and over again he cursed himself for deciding to take that fateful Sunday morning walk.

When Whitley made a late night phone call Simon's speech was slurred and his mood was angry.

"Hello Mr. Lake, sorry to call you at this late hour."

"So you bloody should be. When do I get my car back?"

"Soon sir, but actually I just needed to check something with you regarding your car. Can you confirm that you had it serviced on 15th December?"

"Bloody hell, what are you going to do now, give me a ticket for a bald tyre?"

"No sir, it's just a routine check on something."

"Well I don't know the date but yes, I had it serviced a couple of weeks before Christmas."

"Thank you – and can you confirm that you took the car in to the main dealer, Sterling Cowell."

"Yes, I always do. They supplied it."

"And can you confirm that you collected it on the afternoon of the same day?"

"Yes, why? Where the hell is all this leading, Whitley?"

"Oh it's all just part of our enquiries Mr. Lake. Sorry to bother you – good night, sir."

Simon slammed the phone down so hard that Pippa wondered if he might have broken it. She really felt for him – she knew that he could never ever harm anyone, let alone commit murder. She was so sure of him that she really would have staked her life on it. He had always been a loving husband to her and a good father to their children.

If anything, she thought he was too soft – too emotional, easily upset and unhappy about what he perceived to be a gradual lowering of standards in everyday life. He didn't want to be labelled as a grumpy old man but he did worry about quite where the modern world was heading.

Pippa had first met Simon at a charity ball and was immediately taken by his natural charm and easygoing manner. They were married within a year and there had never been a day when she'd regretted it. Over the years the slim, dark-haired Simon had gone grey and filled out a bit, but to Pippa he had always remained the man she first met.

He'd got more patient and tolerant with age. When she first met him he would sulk for days when his beloved Ipswich football team lost. He was still a season ticket holder but now he could shrug off the defeats – and there were plenty of them – more easily. Sometimes Pippa went with him to home games and they developed friendships with their fellow sufferers who all sat in the same seats, near theirs, year after year.

She had watched him build his career as an accountant and had supported him when he teamed up with Peter Chambers and Chris Bradwell in the new partnership. In the early days they sacrificed a lot to invest both time and money in establishing the firm, but eventually it had all been worthwhile. The client base had grown steadily and the firm's success enabled them to live a comfortable life. Now that the children had grown up and Pippa had left work they had more time for each other. They ate out regularly, took at least two foreign holidays a year, played golf, walked, went to the theatre and generally enjoyed themselves.

It was painful for her now to watch him in such anguish. He didn't deserve it – he'd done the right thing in trying to revive the girl and then calling the police. Now it seemed that DI Whitley really did consider him to be a prime suspect. Pippa prayed on her knees that night that the murderer would soon be caught so that Simon could be cleared and life could return to how it used to be.

At first light the following morning they were both woken by the arrival of the police – for the second morning running. Again it was Whitley who confronted Simon at the front door, and he had his formal face on.

"Simon Jacob Lake, I am arresting you on suspicion of the murder of Kelly Anne Taylor. You do not have to say anything, but it may harm your defence if you fail to mention when questioned something which you later rely on in court. Anything you do say will be given in evidence."

Simon heard Pippa's sudden intake of breath behind him, but he was speechless.
Whitley said, "We need to take you to the station now, Mr. Lake."
He nodded, too numb to speak.

Pippa fought back the tears as she fetched his coat. "Shall I call John Black, darling?"
He nodded again. "Yes, I think that would probably be a very good idea."
"Give me a call as soon as you can. If you need anything at all just let me know. I want you home again just as soon as possible."
He smiled bleakly and kissed her before easing himself in to the waiting police car.

Sat in the interview room with a cup of tea, he wanted an explanation from Whitley. John Black had arrived and he sat by Simon's side. It was the same room he'd been in before but now there was a tape recorder on the desk and on a side table was a TV and a VCR.

"This is just bloody desperation Whitley. You're not getting anywhere with the enquiry and the media are hassling you so you arrest your only suspect. It's just a bloody PR job isn't it?"

Whitley shook his head. "No, Mr. Lake, it isn't. Something has come to light that has forced me to do this."

He switched on the tape recorder and went through the formalities before starting the interview.

"Have you ever met Kelly Taylor prior to finding her body?"

"No, you know I haven't – we've been through that umpteen times."

"We have found something that links you to her and we have irrefutable evidence that you have indeed met her before, Mr. Lake."

"You can't have. I've certainly never knowingly met her. She might have served me in a florist shop sometime or something equally tenuous, but I have never knowingly met the girl."

"You have something in common with Kelly Taylor; you both drive BMWs."

"So what? Lots of people drive BMWs."

"You both had your cars serviced at Sterling Cowell."

"Well, they are the main dealer – it's the obvious place to go for any BMW driver in the Ipswich area."

Whitley narrowed his eyes. "And you both had your cars serviced on 15th December. It says so on the service reminder stickers that the mechanics placed in both your cars."

Simon took a deep breath and sat back in the chair. "Okay, then, that really is some coincidence – but that's all it is."

Whitley leaned forward, arms folded. "Sterling Cowell's security is very good, Mr. Lake. It has to be with lots of high-value cars on the premises. They have cameras all over the place – on the forecourt, in the showroom, even in the customer waiting area."

Simon was wary. "Where is all this leading?"

"Not only do they have lots of cameras but they have a very efficient recording system. Every tenth frame is saved onto tape and then they keep the tapes for three months before recycling them. They had one top end of the range car stolen about a year ago and from their tapes we were able to clearly identify the thief checking it out in the showroom the day before it was taken."

"Okay, all very interesting and commendable, but where the hell are you going with this? What's it got to do with me?"

Whitley switched on the TV and VCR. "I want you to watch this very closely, Mr. Lake. It is CCTV footage of the Sterling Cowell customer waiting area on 15th December. You will see the date and time shown at the bottom of the screen."

He leaned forward, watching intently. He saw the easy chairs, the centre table with newspapers and magazines neatly laid out and the side table with coffee machine, cups and saucers. He also saw four people sitting there.

Whitley paused the tape and pointed to one of the seated figures.

"Can you identify this person, Mr. Lake?"

"Yes, it's me. I remember now – I'd been to Sudbury to see a client with one of the other partners and he dropped me off at Sterling Cowell on our way back to the office. They had just finished the service and I had a coffee while they were preparing the bill."

Whitley nodded and pointed to one of the other waiting customers, a female. "And can you please identify this person, Mr. Lake?"

Simon stared intently at the screen. "Bloody hell, is it Kelly Taylor?"

"It is, Mr. Lake. Attractive girl, wasn't she?"

He looked more closely. She looked different – the hair was different and she was wearing a leather jacket, a short skirt and knee length boots. He gasped as he remembered – he'd spoken to her.

Simon looked aghast at Whitley. "I do remember her now – she spoke to me."

Whitley nodded. "We know she did. The video footage clearly shows you both talking to each other and both of you smiling. You certainly looked like you knew one another."

He shook his head firmly. "No, it wasn't like that. She'd helped herself to a cup of coffee and she remarked that it was nice to have real coffee out of a cup and saucer. I laughed and said that we all paid for the little extras in our BMW service bills. She told me she used to have a Fiesta and when she had that serviced all she got was instant coffee in a plastic cup out of a machine. She laughed and said it tasted foul AND she had to pay for it."

Whitley stared into Simon's face. "So you remember the conversation well. Do pretty young girls often chat to you like that?"

"No, but it was all so innocent – we were both waiting for our cars and she was just making a little bit of idle conversation. Why would a young girl feel she couldn't chat in that situation? If you trace the other people on the screen they'd probably remember and can back me up."

"We're trying to do just that sir."

Whitley put his head on one side, as if to emphasise that he was deep in thought. "Would you call her a sexy girl, Mr. Lake?"

Simon felt himself redden. "I guess so – she was pretty and confident. My main impression was simply that she seemed like a nice person."

"Didn't it strike you that she was dressed sexily – the miniskirt and the boots?"

"Yes, I guess so – but I'm old enough to be her father, for heavens sake."

Whitley was obviously following a particular course of questioning. "From our enquiries so far it seems that Kelly Taylor was attracted to older men, particularly to well-off older men."

Simon looked baffled. "What do you mean?"

"Exactly that – she had been seen in the company of older men. As a florist she was earning just £6.50 an hour for a 40-hour week. She rarely worked overtime and she didn't have any other obvious means of income so far as we know. We are wondering how she could afford to own and drive a BMW on that sort of money."

Simon leaned forward, chin out. "Well … check it out, man. Look at her bank account, see where the payments into her account came from. Check with Sterling Cowell to find out how she paid for the car when she bought it, assuming she did pay for it. If she didn't then find out who did. It's not rocket science, for God's sake."

Whitley leaned back. "We have been doing just that, Mr. Lake. She paid for the car with a banker's draft from her own personal account. Apart from her monthly wages and a few very nominal amounts, there were very few cheques ever paid into her account. However, there were a number of quite large cash payments – two for £5,000 and several more four-figure deposits."

Simon took this in. "Do you think she had a sugar daddy?"

"Yes, at least one and possibly more."

"Well, I certainly wasn't one of them. You can check out my finances in great detail – as a chartered accountant I'm scrupulous about my book-keeping, both in the office and in my personal life."

Whitley looked pensive. "I'm sure that you are, Mr. Lake, and I'm sure you're very adept at keeping all your finances looking neat and tidy. No doubt you have to spend a lot of time helping your clients avoid tax."

"Yes, I help them avoid tax but not evade tax – there's an important distinction between the two. Tax avoidance is legal and tax evasion isn't."

He looked at John Black and then back at Whitley. "What do you really think Kelly Taylor was doing? Did she have a rich boyfriend or do you think she was working as an escort girl or something?"

"I don't know. We are keeping an open mind but when a 22-year-old florist is paying thousands in cash into her bank account it seems unusual, to say the least."

Simon placed both hands palm down on the table and leaned forward purposefully. "Well, I can tell you, Whitley, that as a chartered accountant, if I was giving her bundles of cash for some illicit reason I would advise her on what to do with it and it certainly wouldn't be to pay it in to a current account. I would make sure she hid it in a smarter way than that."

"Yes, I'm sure you'd know how to do that, Mr. Lake, and I'm sure you would be equally careful not to leave an audit trail for any illicit spending that you might have."

Black interjected. "This is really not acceptable, Detective Inspector. My client is being totally cooperative and completely reasonable. You have absolutely no grounds for even suspecting my client has any illicit spending – he is a highly respected professional man with an unblemished record."

Whitley smiled and sat back. "Of course. I think that's enough for now. Interview suspended at 1132."

CHAPTER 6

Simon was left alone with Black and they had a chance to talk.

"What do you think, John? What's going on?"

"I think the DI is clutching at straws. They probably don't have any other suspects yet and they've decided to give you a bit of a grilling. To be fair, they have to, given that you found her body shortly after the time of death."

"So what are you saying, exactly?"

"Only that they don't have any concrete evidence against you and they're trying to find some."

"Whitley said she'd been seen in the company of older men – why don't they trace them?"

"No doubt they're working on that. If she was working as an escort girl there might be lots of suspects. The money could have come from multiple clients and she saved it up. Maybe she did have a rich sugar daddy who looked after her and made sure she kept the affair secret with presents of cash. One thing is for sure, though, Whitley will have plenty of people out there doing the legwork to find out just what she got up to outside of that florist shop. They'll soon turn something up and then Whitley will have other suspects to pester."

Simon gazed at the ceiling. "What I just can't understand is why on earth she would be on the Ganges site on a winter's morning. She would hardly be meeting a client to provide sexual services in the open air on a freezing cold Sunday morning, would she?"

"No, but she might have had a rendezvous with someone, perhaps. Maybe someone was handing over some cash and things went wrong."

He sighed. "Whoever it was must have got out of there bloody fast – I didn't see a soul and I was keeping an eye out all the time in case there was a security guard around."

"We can only speculate, but try not to worry. They can't charge you without any evidence. My guess is that they'll release you soon."

"Can you call Pippa and let her know what's happening? Tell her I'm okay and there's no point in her coming here. Say that I hope to be home soon."

John put his hand on Simon's arm. "By now the media will know you've been arrested and there will be an army of reporters at your house. Your name will be on the TV and radio news, I'm afraid – and in the evening papers."

Simon slumped forward, head in hands. "Bloody hell, what a nightmare. Everyone will assume I did it."

"Some will… just until the real culprit is found. Look, I'll make sure Pippa is okay. Is there someone who can keep her company … or can she go and stay with someone to get her away from the media?"

"She could stay with our son Paul, he only lives an hour away in Cambridge. Will they let me call him to explain?"

"Don't worry, give me his number and I'll contact him right after I've spoken to Pippa."

A PC brought Simon a mug of coffee and a sandwich and then posted himself outside the door. Simon ate slowly while he tried to take in just what was happening to him. He thought about Pippa and how scared she must be. He thought about the children and how shocked they would be. He thought about his friends, everyone in the office, the clients. Everyone would be talking – wondering if he would be capable of murdering a young girl.

He had always been comfortable with himself and he thought that other people were comfortable around him. He got on well with both clients and staff and he had no skeletons in the cupboard. He'd been faithful to Pippa and although he still looked at beautiful women in the street, all he ever did was look. He had once snogged Janice, sometimes unkindly referred to as the office bike, in a drunken moment at a Christmas party, but that was hardly a hanging offence.

He realised that the nightmare would go on until the killer was found. Even if they released him soon, he knew the speculation would go on until all this was resolved. Pippa and the children, and John, would all know for certain that he was totally innocent – but what about everyone else? He felt sure his partners Peter and Chris would have total faith in him, as would most of the people in the office. In fact, he felt sure that everyone who had known him for some time would find it impossible to believe he could be capable of murder.

Those who didn't really know him or were only acquaintances would be sure to wonder, to speculate, to gossip with each other. He wondered how smart the police were – how smart Whitley was. What chance was there of them getting to the bottom of this?

John came back in and tried to provide some reassurance. The police had cordoned off the house and were doing their best to turn away onlookers. The neighbours were looking after Pippa and warding off the reporters. She had spoken to both the children and consequently son Paul had dropped everything and was now on his way over from Cambridge. The house had been shown on all the lunchtime TV news programmes so there was no hope of his identity being kept under wraps.

The interviewing continued in the afternoon – going over and over the finding of the body and the meeting with Kelly at the BMW dealer's. When Whitley finally said that was enough, he thought he would be going home.

"So, can I go? Your 24 hours will be up first thing in the morning."

"No I'm afraid not," said Whitley. "We've been granted an extension, so you'll be spending the night here."

Simon was body searched and had to empty the contents of his pockets. He handed over his belt and shoes before he was led into a cell and the door was slammed and locked behind him. He sat on the bed in the bare cell and wondered how the hell he had been reduced to this.

What followed was probably the worst night of his life. He had almost no sleep due to a combination of worry and a drunk in the next cell shouting incessantly. He was relieved when a PC finally brought him a mug of tea early in the morning.

After a half-hearted breakfast of tea and toast, John Black arrived.

"Morning, Simon. How are you bearing up?"

"Bloody awful. What a night. What's happening?"

"Well, I've just seen Whitley and he wants to ask you some more questions, but I think you'll be out of here soon. I just can't see that he's got any grounds to charge you. The only reason you were arrested was because of the video footage."

"Have you spoken to Pippa this morning?"

"Yes, just now. Paul is with her – he wanted to take her back to Cambridge but she wouldn't have it. Said she wanted to be at home ready for you coming back."

"What are they saying about me in the media?"

"Oh, only what you would expect. I'm afraid your name and address and occupation are all out in the open. Reporters have been quizzing your neighbours and some of the staff at the office."

"What are they all saying?"

"Only good stuff – nice respectable man, nobody can believe you would be guilty of something like this."

"Do they know anything of the BMW connection?"

"No, nobody seems to have got that. The general gist is that you are under suspicion largely because you were the person who found the body."

"Well, let's hope I will be going home soon. What if they charge me?"

"Try not to worry, Simon. Unless they come up with something we don't know about then I can't see how they could."

John proved to be right. Following another session going over the same ground that they had covered the day before, Whitley finally gave him the good news – he was free to go home.

He stood up. "So what happens now?"

"We continue our enquiries, Mr. Lake. We will need to know your whereabouts as we may well need to speak to you some more."

Simon was angry. "So you arrested me when you could have simply carried on questioning me. I've been totally cooperative but now my name is in all the papers. Why did you have to do it?"

"I'm sorry sir, but we needed unrestricted access to you while we questioned you in detail."

Simon stared at him. "So are you satisfied now or do you really think I did it?"

"I honestly don't know, Mr. Lake. I have to keep an open mind and we will continue our enquiries. What I can tell you is that I am totally convinced we will catch the killer eventually."

"Well I hope you do, because you've put me and my family through hell. All because I had the misfortune to find a dead body – no wonder people are wary of reporting anything to the police."

Whitley returned his stare. "I'm sorry sir, but we have to do our job."

"What about my car, can I have that back now?"

"Yes sir, it's outside. I'll get the keys from the desk sergeant."

"I'd like to phone home first. My son is with my wife and I want him to be ready to open the gates for me so I can get in quick and then we can get the door closed to all those bloody reporters ASAP."

When he arrived home there was a frenzy of activity as reporters tried to block his path and get a word from him. Paul had roped in two of the neighbours to help and they literally had to barge people aside so that Simon could drive in. The garage doors were open and he drove straight in while Paul closed the gates and the garage doors. Simon used the connecting door from the garage to enter the house.

He embraced Pippa as if they'd been apart for months. She was crying and hugging him and repeatedly telling him everything would be okay now.
He held her at arm's length. "I don't think so. The media will hound us, people will wonder if I did it and I don't think life will be much fun until they catch whoever did do it."

"Well, I know you didn't do it and all the people who are important to us know you didn't do it. We can't stop other people thinking whatever the media lead them to think."
Paul embraced his dad. "I'm here for as long as I can help, Dad. I believe in you one hundred per cent, always have and always will."
Simon felt his eyes moisten. He suspected he was going to need all the support he could get over the next few days and perhaps weeks.

They watched the BBC News 24 channel and it seemed bizarre to see the house live on TV. They showed footage of Simon arriving home and Paul closing the gate. Somehow they'd got hold of a photograph of him – he recognised it as one taken recently at a cocktail reception held by one of their clients. A reporter was standing by the gate explaining how the man arrested yesterday had now been released and was back at home in the house behind him. He said the police had confirmed that Simon Lake, a chartered accountant, was still helping them with their enquiries but that he had not been charged with any offence.

Paul took all the incoming phone calls and filtered them according to whether he figured Simon would want to talk. His sister Chloe called and asked to speak to her dad. She was very emotional and between the tears she told him she loved him and that she would do absolutely anything for him. She wanted to come over but he told her to stay at home in London until things settled down. It was bad enough seeing his face on national TV – he didn't want the rest of the family exposed.

Peter called from the office. "Hi Simon, glad to hear you are back home. How are you, old man?"

"I've been better. The bloody police never needed to have arrested me. They've had to let me go because they've got no evidence. It seems that I'm a suspect just because I found her."

"Well, we never doubted you for one second. Everyone here sends their best wishes and we are all looking forward to seeing you back again."

"Okay, at least that's good to hear. I'm going to stay here for now though, as I don't want to leave Pippa on her own trying to fend off the reporters."

"Yeah sure, just do whatever you think is best."

"I'll get back to working on Dalton's stuff soon, Peter, but my head is all over the place right now. I just need the police to make some headway with finding the killer."

"Well, just give me a call any time if you need anything. Don't worry at all about anything in the office. We're coping fine and I'll tell Charles Dalton you'll be back on his year-end soon."

Simon walked up the stairs to the main bedroom and peered out of a crack in the curtains. The bedroom looked out on to the front gate and the roadway. There were a group of reporters standing around hopefully, but because Paul had locked the gates this kept them out on the pavement.

He saw various people walking slowly past, staring at the house, hoping for a glimpse of something they could gossip about. He saw the large Indian woman who lived four doors away actually pass the house four times. Even the traffic was slowing down as drivers peered at the house.

Simon wondered if the house would be forever known as the place where that suspected killer lived. He wondered if it would ever again be the comfortable family home that he and Pippa had loved so much. He wondered if they'd have to move house once this was all over. Would some people see him in a different light even after the killer was eventually brought to justice?

He was at least pleased that the security was good. They had an expensive alarm system and they were able to floodlight the outside of the house. He had no intention of allowing the situation to drive them out of the house – he wanted his life back again.

The three of them sat down to a proper meal that evening in the dining room. Simon wondered if they should go out to eat, to spare Pippa the work of preparing something, but she insisted on cooking and made a chicken stir-fry. He knew it was probably best not to run the risk of being recognised and being stared at by fellow diners. Paul did his level best to lift their spirits and a bottle of Sauvignon Blanc helped.

They drank brandy after the meal and that night Simon had his best sleep of the week. He awoke in the morning in a more positive mood, but this was short-lived. One glance at the front page of the paper ruined any feelings of optimism.

CHAPTER 7

Right there on the front page, under a headline of 'Murdered Girl Knew Man Who Found Her Body', was a picture taken from the Sterling Cowell CCTV footage. It was poor quality, probably from a camera phone, but it showed a smiling Kelly talking to Simon.

The text explained that the picture was taken in the customer area of a BMW dealership in Ipswich. It didn't explain what was being said but stated that the two were captured on film talking to each other. The picture looked bad as it showed Kelly sitting down with her legs crossed. Her short skirt revealed lots of thigh, and she looked as if she was showing Simon her best assets.

Simon was slumped in a chair at the dinette table when Pippa came downstairs.
She looked over his shoulder. "Oh my God."
Simon looked up. "Looks bloody awful, doesn't it?"
She nodded. "How the hell have the media got hold of this?"
 "Oh it's somebody making a quick buck. Probably some toe-rag using their mobile to take a picture off a screen and then phoning the papers."
 "It's dreadful … just dreadful."

The phone rang. It was John. "Have you seen the papers?"
 "Yes, we're just looking at it."
 "I'm sorry, but to be honest this was bound to come out. I wasn't surprised. The tabloid hacks are so savvy these days – if there's anything out there they'll find it somehow or other."
 "It just looks so bloody bad. People will assume that now they've found some sort of link, however tenuous, it really does point the finger firmly at me."

"You just have to ride this out. All we can do is hope the police make some rapid progress."

"I'm not at all optimistic. I haven't seen any signs that they have a clue. I have a horrible feeling that they're so sure it was me they might not be looking too hard for anyone else."

"No, I don't believe that. That's not how a murder investigation works. They will have lots of people working very hard on this. Whitley will make sure none of them just sit back and assume that all they have to do is prove that it was you".

"I hope you're right, but I haven't heard any mention of progress in other directions."

"No, well I don't think you would. They'll keep that to themselves and they'll want you to feel nervous and unsure in the hope that if it was you then you'll make a mistake and let something slip."

"Well they've certainly succeeded in making me nervous and unsure - I'm bloody terrified."

"I know, you're bound to be but all you can do is keep your head down. Call me anytime if anything develops."

Simon went up to the bedroom and peered out of the chink in the curtains. His heart sank; there were even more reporters out there than the day before. They were all huddled in groups and there were two TV vans with satellite dishes parked right outside.

Paul came in to the room and put his arm round his dad's shoulders. "We need to just stay indoors, Dad. If we keep the curtains closed and don't answer the door they'll eventually give up."

Simon turned to look at him. "Prisoners in our own home – what a bloody nightmare."

Simon was unable to do anything other than watch and listen to the news channels. The phone rang a number of times and Paul took every call. He suspected that some hacks had got hold of their number and he refused to talk to anyone he wasn't one hundred per cent convinced about. Simon only spoke to Chloe, John Black and the office.

He made countless trips upstairs to peer out of the curtains and took to counting the people outside. The average was fourteen and it wasn't going down. Lots of locals seemed to be giving their pets an inordinate amount of exercise – he figured that there would be a lot of tired dogs in the neighbourhood come the end of the day.

By mid-afternoon Simon felt so useless and frustrated that he called Whitley at the police station.

"Hello, it's Simon Lake here. Can't you give me any news? I'm stuck here in the house just hiding from the bloody press."

"Oh, hello Mr. Lake. All I can really tell you is that we are working very hard on our enquiries and I promise you we will leave no stone unturned."

"But are you actually getting anywhere? Do you have any suspects?"

"Well, we have been following up with the customers and staff who were at Sterling Cowell on the day you met Kelly."

"Bloody hell, Whitley – the day I met Kelly! You make it sound like I had some sort of prearranged assignation with her. It was a ten-second conversation about the coffee, for God's sake. What the hell are you doing about following up other angles?"

"Mr. Lake, I assure you we have to check out everything. We are also talking to the manager and the staff at the shop where she worked and we are talking to her bank. We've knocked on the door of just about every house in Shotley. I promise you we are working as hard as we possibly can. We're all working very long days – I only had about four hours sleep last night."

Simon retorted, "Well, that's a lot more than I bloody had", and slammed the phone down.

When he had calmed down a little and thought about what Whitley had said, he did actually feel a tiny bit better about things. If they were going into the details of Kelly's finances and talking to the girls at the shop then surely something would come to light. The girls were bound to gossip between them about what they did outside of work and about their boyfriends. Also they would be bound to think long and hard about their different customers and whether they might ever have seen Kelly's killer in the shop.

Simon was less optimistic about the door-to-door checks they'd been making in Shotley. The case had received such huge publicity that anyone who had seen anything of any use would surely have come forward by now. He couldn't imagine that somebody would suddenly remember they'd taken their dog for a walk around the Ganges site at the crucial time.

He supposed there was a remote possibility that someone might have been reluctant to come forward because they didn't want to admit they'd been trespassing. The police had been stressing that this was of no concern to them – with a murder enquiry under way they certainly weren't worried about somebody walking their dog where they shouldn't.

The frustrating thing was that there was only one main road leading out to the Shotley peninsula and on a Sunday morning there was so little traffic on that road. There would have been a few locals making the journey to and from Ipswich or collecting their Sunday paper, perhaps a few people heading for the marina to work on their boats, but nobody much else. There was a foot ferry that operated between Shotley and the ports of Harwich and Felixstowe but this didn't even run in the middle of winter.

It was almost certain that the killer either went to Shotley by car or actually lived in Shotley. The private boat traffic in and out of the marina was minimal at this time of year. There was a lock through which boats had to pass and this was under constant supervision. Surely the police would be talking to the lock keeper. Simon figured that somebody could have been sleeping on a boat in the marina but if they did then the lock-keeper was likely to know.

The population of Shotley Gate village was probably no more than a couple of thousand. Simon knew that in all probability nobody had taken any notice of the few cars that travelled along that road on that particular morning. There were no speed cameras that he knew of. There were footpaths that led to Shotley along the banks of the rivers Orwell and Stour but the killer was hardly likely to be a rambler.

The more he thought about it, the more Simon became convinced that the comment from Whitley about Kelly being seen with older men could well be the key to everything. Maybe she was working as an escort or maybe she had a sugar daddy. Maybe she was pushing her sugar daddy towards leaving his wife and he had to silence her. The possibilities were endless. Simon really needed the police to get somewhere, and soon.

By the end of the afternoon the number of reporters outside was down to eleven and they looked really fed up, stamping their feet and swinging their arms, trying to keep warm. He hoped the weather would be as bad as possible to drive them all away. The phone was ringing more frequently now as more and more of the media somehow obtained the number. Pippa decided she'd had enough and took the phone off the hook, reasoning that anyone they really wanted to talk to had their mobile numbers.

He logged in to his email account and was horrified to find over two hundred new unread messages. Every single one that was from an address he didn't recognise he deleted without bothering to read. He then trawled through the websites of all the national daily papers. Predictably the broadsheet's reports were mostly factual and the tabloids were sensational.

The tabloid message was that the police had uncovered a secret link between Simon Lake and Kelly Taylor. The suggestion was that this was something he had tried to cover up but he had been caught out. The inference of guilt was obvious. Simon slumped in his chair.

He found himself peering out of the curtains more and more frequently – partly to count the number of media people outside and partly to check that the police weren't coming to re-arrest him. A few of the neighbours had come to the door, enquiring whether they could help and perhaps relishing the media attention. Paul turned them all away politely, saying that they just wanted to keep their heads down and not do anything to arouse the interest of the press.

Come the following morning the number of media people outside had dwindled to four and the television vans had gone. Simon started to wonder if he could go out but Paul and Pippa quickly talked him out of it, convincing him that the time to go out was when all of the hacks had given up.

Being confined to the house was having an adverse affect on both Simon and Pippa. He half-heartedly did a bit of spreadsheet work on Charles Dalton's books but kept breaking off to search the net and see what the media were saying about him. He looked at some of the chatroom stuff relating to the news and was dismayed to see emails from people questioning why Simon Lake was free and hadn't been charged already.

Pippa was also showing the pressure and it was Paul who was keeping things together. Both Simon and Pippa knew they were relying on him but that he had a job to do and couldn't stay with them indefinitely. Chloe wanted to come and help, but with small children to look after and a busy husband abroad on business, they insisted that she stay put.

When Simon checked the front of the house the following morning he was delighted to see nobody outside.

Pippa looked over his shoulder. "They've gone, darling, you're not headline news any more. Maybe we can try getting back to something like normal."

Simon shook his head. "No chance, people still suspect me and it will all get stirred up again when Kelly's funeral takes place. This won't end until they find the killer."

Simon showered and shaved and then announced that he was going out.

Pippa looked at him, concerned. "Is that wise?"

"I've got to, darling. I can't stay cooped up in here forever. I'm just going to get the car out and drive to the shop to get the papers. I want to see what the tabloids are saying about me today."

He was back twenty minutes later looking just as forlorn.

Pippa was anxious. ""How are you?"

"Invisible, it seems. The girl in the shop looked at me like I was an alien but everyone else blanked me. I saw Roy from down the road and Sally Jones, but when I went to say good morning they just looked the other way. It's like I've got some sort of deadly disease."

"People are bound to feel awkward."

"What do you mean? Awkward about talking to a murder suspect?"

Pippa looked down. "I know how you must be feeling."

"Do you? How the hell could you? Have you ever been suspected of committing a murder? Of course you don't bloody know how I feel."

Pippa took herself off to the kitchen for refuge while Simon shut himself in his study. After an hour of pacing around and achieving absolutely nothing, Simon was determined to get out again.
He shouted, "I'm off to the office", and walked out without even checking that Pippa or Paul had heard him. The two of them met in the hall – Paul stopping her from following Simon.
"Just leave him, Mum. Maybe it will do him good to get back to the office – the longer he leaves it the harder it will be."

When Simon breezed in to the office, trying his best to pretend it was just a normal working day, he met with a mixed reaction. Peter was clearly delighted to see him, as was Jo, who provided secretarial services to all three partners. Everyone else seemed unsure what to say or do – he felt like he had walked in to a room where everyone had just been discussing him.

He needed some of Charles Dalton's paperwork photocopying – Jo was busy with Peter and so he asked Sally, one of the office juniors, to do it for him. She blushed and averted her eyes, mumbling that yes, of course she would do it.

He went into the kitchen to make himself a mug of coffee and the three people in there mumbled hellos and promptly found something more urgent they needed to do.

He shut himself in his office and started working through the backlog of emails and messages. After an hour or so Peter knocked at the door and entered. "So, how are you bearing up, old man?"

He shrugged. "It's bloody awkward, Peter – I'm developing a siege mentality. This is the first day I've been out for a while. I went to the paper shop and everyone blanked me and it's much the same here. All I want to do is to get back in to the normal routine but it's so bloody difficult."

"I know – and it's bound to be at first. You just need some time to pass and for the police to get somewhere."

Simon stared at the carpet. "What if they don't get anywhere? What if they've already made as much progress as they're ever going to? Will they keep trying or will they figure they need to nail the one and only suspect they've got?"

"You can't think like that. It's still early days. Come the end of the week they could have the murderer locked up and everyone feeling sorry for what you've been through."

"Or they could have got nowhere and have decided to charge me – I could be locked up."

Peter put his hand on his shoulder. "I know you are in the clear and so does everyone close to you. Only people who don't know you might be wondering, and you can't stop that."

"Well, if that's true why can't people in the office talk to me? Everyone's avoiding me like the plague."

"Not because they suspect you, Simon. It's only because they feel awkward. They know it was an awful thing that happened and that you're going through a tough time. They don't know whether you want to talk or what."

"Well I'm going to take some more stuff home and try to get really stuck in to Dalton's bloody year-end. Can you reassure him that I haven't forgotten about him – I just don't want to get into a long conversation."

"Yes, sure – don't worry about it."

"We have to worry about it, he's our biggest client. We can't have him walking away from us because he thinks I can't handle it with everything else that's going on."

Back at home that night Simon received a call from DI Whitley. "Mr. Lake, I just wanted to tell you that the post-mortem on Kelly Taylor has been completed and the findings confirm that death was caused by constriction to the neck. We can't release the body for burial yet but a funeral service will take place at Ipswich Cemetery next Wednesday at 2 pm. There will be a further family-only service later on when the actual burial takes place."

"Oh, I see. I don't suppose it would be a good idea for me to attend? As the person who found her I would like to be there, but as you and the media have put a cloud of suspicion over me it would be very awkward."

"Er, yes. I wouldn't recommend it. I would suggest you just lie low and if you like I can have an officer on duty outside your house on the day."

"Do you think that's necessary? What do you think might happen?"

"Well, sometimes friends and relatives can get very emotional in this sort of situation and some hothead might go looking for someone to vent their anger on."

"Well you know that the best solution for everyone would be if you got your finger out and found the killer. That would make both Kelly's family and me and my family feel a whole lot better."

"Yes sir, I realise that and I assure you we are continuing to work very hard at doing just that."

"Look, can I come in and see you to talk about what's happening with your enquiries? I'm worried that you're not getting anywhere and I might have some ideas on how you might pursue some other avenues."

"No, I'm sorry sir, but that really wouldn't be right and proper. You have to leave this to us and we will contact you if we think that you can help us."

"All I want to know is that you really are pursuing every angle. I know that I am totally innocent but my life and the lives of all my family are being ruined by all this uncertainty and speculation. I want to help you prove my innocence by finding whoever did this."

"Yes, I know you do and I appreciate your cooperation, but you have to leave it to us."

"You mean you can't collude with someone who you still regard as a suspect?"

"To be blunt, Mr. Lake, yes."

CHAPTER 8

When Simon got up the following morning he found a folded sheet of lined paper on the doormat underneath the Daily Telegraph. He spread it out on the kitchen table. In crude block capitals it spelt out: "WHY DON'T YOU JUST OWN UP YOU BASTARD".

He opened the curtains and stared at the frost-covered lawn, wondering bleakly if this nightmare would ever end.

Paul came down and saw the message before Simon had a chance to bin it.

"Don't take any notice, Dad. It's just some nutter."

"Is it? It might be from a neighbour, or one of Kelly's family. Maybe most of the people in Ipswich are convinced it's me."

Paul shook his head. "No, don't think like that. You've got to keep things in perspective."

Pippa appeared at the kitchen door. "What is it? What's happened?"

Simon grabbed the piece of paper and screwed it up but she took it from him, smoothed it out and read it. She shook her head sadly as she threw it in the bin.

Pippa made coffee and the three of them sat at the dinette table staring into space.

Paul eventually broke the silence. "Do you suppose there are any cameras covering the road out to Shotley?"

Simon shook his head. "No, I've already thought about that. I don't think there's a single speed camera on that road and even if there was I guess it would only be activated by someone exceeding the limit."

Paul wasn't convinced. "The Orwell bridge spans that road. Maybe that has some sort of camera. If there was a camera covering the river it might also show cars on the road where it skirts the riverbank."

Simon wasn't optimistic. "Anyway, the killer wouldn't necessarily go along that stretch of the road. There is a turning from Holbrook on to the Shotley road at Freston. From Freston out to Shotley there are also a few minor roads leading to tiny villages."

Paul wouldn't let it drop. "Yes, but I bet that at least ninety per cent of the cars that go to Shotley travel along the main road from Ipswich and go under the Orwell bridge. It's worth checking out."

Simon nodded. "Okay, I'll mention it to Whitley."

Paul made some calls to his office and was studying his diary. "I can stay until Sunday but I'll have to go home then. I've got a client meeting on Monday that I just can't get out of."

Simon understood. "Yes, of course. We're just grateful that you've stayed this long. You've been brilliant, Paul, but your old Dad is going to have to stand on his own two feet now and see this through."

"I'll only be at the end of the phone. Call me any time - and you Mum."

The weekend passed without further incident. Although there was still plenty of local news coverage and speculation over the murder enquiry, the national media had moved on to other things. The next hurdle was to get through Kelly's funeral. Simon wondered about her family – how her Mum and Dad and the rest of the family were coping. He would have liked to talk to them and find out more about her but he knew that it was out of the question.

When Paul departed on the Sunday both Simon and Pippa felt lonely and vulnerable. They decided they needed a change of scenery and some fresh air so they drove up to Aldeburgh, a pretty little town further up the Suffolk coast. Over the years it had become a popular bolthole for well-heeled Londoners who could afford a second home by the sea. They parked by the seafront and walked hand in hand along the beach, trying to clear their heads. Simon felt that he was behaving like a detective, constantly thinking things through and trying to find a new angle that would lead to the killer. He knew that Pippa was doing the same but she was keeping her thoughts very much to herself.

They had dinner at The Old Lighthouse, one of their favourite restaurants. Over a plate of fresh seafood and a good bottle of Chablis, he started to feel a little better. He wondered if Paul might be onto something with his idea of possible camera coverage of the road to Shotley. He tried to convince himself that the police might have found something and were perhaps knocking on the killer's door right now.

They both felt better on the drive back home but their mood was very different once they had put the car in the garage and went to open the front door. Painted roughly on the door was the single word: 'MURDERER'.

The paint was still wet. Simon went back in the garage and emerged with a bottle of white spirits and a rag.
Pippa put her hand on his arm. "Should you do that? Shouldn't we get the police to check it out?"
Simon shrugged her off. "What's the bloody point – they won't do anything. If they can't catch a murderer they won't put much effort in to finding a graffiti-daubing yob."

Pippa watched her husband in despair. He rubbed the door like his life depended on it, threw the rag in the bin, put the white spirit back in the garage and then stormed into the house. She wasn't a religious woman but that night she did pray for him.

The approach of the funeral rekindled the media's interest in the case. Following the graffiti incident Simon took up Whitley's offer of a PC watching the house until the day after the funeral.

He also contacted a local security firm who came and installed additional intruder lights all around the house and a device that emitted a loud bleeping noise whenever anyone opened the front gate or approached any of the exterior doors. While they were there he also had them service the burglar alarm system.

Simon did get excited when he tackled Whitley on the camera issue, but this was soon dampened. It seemed they had already been checking this angle and had found that there was indeed a camera on the bridge and they kept video footage for a period of one month. Unfortunately this was primarily to cover activity on the river area and not on the road. It did show part of the road but not well enough to read the number plates of any of the vehicles travelling along it.

They had been studying the footage at great length, though, and enhancing some of the images in more detail. From this they believed they had identified both Simon's and Kelly's cars travelling from Ipswich towards Shotley on the morning in question. Simon's was timed at 1023 on the Sunday morning and Kelly's at 0938.

They had counted a total of just 116 cars travelling on that road towards Shotley between the hours of 0900 and 1100. It was believed that they could probably identify most of the car types, but not their registration numbers or their colour, as the footage was in black and white. Whitley took the view that it might help them in building up a case against an already-identified suspect but that it wouldn't provide conclusive evidence against anyone.

Assuming that they had correctly identified the cars, then Kelly had been forty-five minutes ahead of Simon. Given that he had wasted little time between parking at Shotley and walking on to the Ganges site, this made the time window very short. Kelly must have parked, walked, met someone and then met her death within a window of probably just forty minutes. Simon wondered if the killer had even seen him approaching and left by a different route. There were many ways on and off the site via the gaps in the perimeter fences that had been created over the years.

Kelly's funeral service was a huge affair, attended by her many friends and family but also by many well-wishers from the local community and others who were simply curious. It received blanket coverage from all the local media and it was also the third item on the main BBC evening news and the second item on both ITN and Sky. Despite the absence of a coffin there were many flowers in evidence.

Simon and Pippa watched all of the coverage, constantly flicking from channel to channel. They were dismayed to see some more coverage of their house and the reminders that Simon Lake, an Ipswich accountant, had found the body and was subsequently arrested, questioned and then released without charge.

The shift of PCs on watch outside the house had all been friendly enough and Pippa had kept them well supplied with tea and biscuits. Whenever anyone dawdled too long outside the house they would be politely but firmly moved on.

Pippa had hoped that Simon might be able to move forward after the funeral, but he showed no signs of lifting himself out of a trough of despair. She knew that while the killer was still at large the attention might lessen over time but it wouldn't go away. She had continued to pray every night that he would soon be caught.

Simon made sporadic efforts to do some work, but no matter how hard he tried he just couldn't concentrate. He took to walking all over the house, peering out of the curtains, checking the news on the TV and radio and watching over the roadway for any sign of unusual activity.

He insisted that Pippa get back to her normal life.

"You haven't been to the golf club since all this started. It would do you good to get out."

She looked uncertain. "I don't know that I want to. It will be awkward for the other girls."

"What do you mean – awkward playing with the wife of a suspected killer?"

"No, you know what I mean. Nobody can behave as if nothing has happened."

"Well, you might have to get used to it. The way things are going the police won't ever catch him. I could be living under this cloud forever."

Pippa touched his arm. "Please don't say that – you've got to have faith, you have to keep believing."

He shrugged her off. "Well, maybe I just can't."

She watched him trudge out of the back door and down to the bottom of the garden, where he shut himself in the summerhouse.

While Pippa was out the loneliness really hit Simon hard. He missed the support of his son Paul, his wife seemed unable to help and the police presence outside had now been withdrawn. He felt that he was completely isolated. He couldn't really go anywhere and yet he didn't want to stay in. He craved normality… stability.

He drove to the local shop and scanned the front pages of the tabloids while he paid his paper bill. The woman behind the counter managed to add up the bill, take his money and give him his change and a receipt, all without actually looking at him. He drove around Ipswich for half an hour, partly for a change of scenery and partly because he didn't want to go back to the house.

When he did return the mail was on the mat. Amongst the bank statements, bills and junk mail was a plain white envelope with his name and address spelt out in large childlike capitals. Inside was a sheet of A4 with just one word on it – 'KILLER'. Simon sat at the dinette table and sobbed.

When Pippa returned she was quiet and Simon knew she hadn't enjoyed her round of golf.

"How did you get on?"

"Oh, so-so. We played Stableford – I got twenty-nine points. Jenny won with thirty-seven."

"What was the chat like on the way round?"

"Stilted is probably the word. Nobody really knows what to say."

"You didn't get a grilling, then?"

"Oh no, quite the opposite. They were sympathetic, asking how we were coping."

Simon didn't really want to know what the people at the golf club were saying. He knew only too well what everyone was wondering – could that nice quiet accountant have a different side to him?

The following morning he decided he just had to get stuck into Charles Dalton's year-end work. He had an accounting package on his PC for the day-to-day stuff and a whole series of spreadsheets for the more arcane things. It was a never-ending job to track that the acquisition and disposal of assets was done in the most tax-efficient way.

There were very large sums of money in a number of offshore accounts and Simon was always trying to stay bang up to date with just where the best rates were. Dalton was always telling him he'd seen something in the FT or The Times that looked better than anything they were using. Simon had to spend a lot of time studying the financial press and all the relevant websites just to keep one step ahead of him.

He stared at the rows and columns of figures, but he wasn't taking anything in. As he tried to dream up new angles of enquiry that he thought the police might not be working on, the figures just became a blur. He thought about the camera on the Orwell Bridge and the relatively small number of cars that had been visible on the Shotley road on that Sunday morning. He wondered how he could get to see that videotape and then he had a thought.

Whitley was in his office when Simon rang. "Hello, it's Simon Lake. I've had an idea which I think might help."
Whitley didn't sound enthusiastic. "Oh, and what's that?"

"I know you've got the tape of the camera footage of the Orwell and the Shotley road. Can I come in and have a look at it? I just figure that it might jog my memory about the cars that were parked near me on the seafront at Shotley that morning."

"The footage is very poor, Mr. Lake. We had great difficulty spotting your car and Kelly's car, and to be honest we're not even certain about them. We can just about identify a dark-coloured 5 series BMW estate, which would match yours, and a light-coloured 3 series that matches Kelly's. We haven't a hope in hell of confirming this by the registration numbers though – it's just that the times and cars seem to fit with what we know."

"Even so, I'd like to come in and have a look. Right now I can't recall anything about any of the cars parked there, but who knows, the tape might trigger something."

"Okay sir, there's no harm in us trying. I should be in until about three."

Simon wasn't optimistic about seeing anything that might help, but at least it would give him a chance to quiz Whitley about just what they were doing.

CHAPTER 9

Simon had to wait to see DI Whitley. The desk sergeant said he was "busy interviewing". Simon wondered briefly if he had another suspect, but this hope was soon dashed. From just eavesdropping on the chatter going on behind the desk it soon became apparent that it was in connection with a betting scam at Newmarket races.

Eventually Whitley appeared and apologised for keeping him waiting.

"I hear you're working on another case?"

"Yes I am, but that doesn't mean we're not still working on the Kelly Taylor case."

"Does it mean you've downgraded it?"

"Not at all. I have officers working on it full time but I'm also involved with other ongoing cases."

"Doesn't a murder enquiry get top priority?"

"We are constantly reviewing all ongoing cases and prioritising the manning of each of them in line with how much work we can do."

"What does that mean – that you're not working hard on Kelly's case because you think you know that I did it?"

"Not at all sir. I promise you we're keeping a completely open mind."

"But it would be very convenient for you if you could prove it was me and then move on to other things?"

"Mr. Lake, we only want to find the person responsible for her murder. We don't charge someone based on probability. We look in every direction when gathering evidence. There are various avenues we are following up but I couldn't possibly tell you about them."

"Does that mean that other people are being checked out and spoken to?"

"I'm sorry, but I'm not prepared to divulge any more."

When they looked at the tape, Simon was really disappointed. The cars were so tiny and indistinct that he couldn't really make out what any of them were. Apart from two lorries, all the other vehicles looked pretty much the same. Whitley had book-marked the frames that showed what they believed were Simon's and Kelly's cars. He said they had done everything they possibly could to enhance every single vehicle image to come up with a probable match.

He looked at Whitley intently. "So have you been able to identify the make and model of all of the cars in the right time-frame?"

"Yes, pretty much. Some we've only been able to identify generically though – a small hatchback or an MPV or whatever. There are so many different cars that look so similar these days."

"But no registration numbers?"

"Unfortunately not, but today we are putting out requests through the media for everyone who made that journey on that morning to contact us just for the purpose of elimination."

"You still don't know for sure that the killer even used that road, though."

"No, that's true. They could have joined the Shotley road at the Holbrook turning or even at one of the little byroads further along. They could have come from the marina or they might actually live in Shotley village. We're not ruling anything out."

Simon wasn't convinced. "Haven't you turned up anything else – surely you must be interviewing some other suspects?"

"No, not at this stage."

"Don't you have any other suspects?"

"I'm not prepared to discuss that, I'm afraid."

"So I just have to sit at home stewing – waiting for the next piece of hate mail or the next graffiti merchant who wants to vandalise my property?"

"Any mail like that you should pass on to us, Mr. Lake, and you should definitely report any act of vandalism to us right away."

"I don't see what good it will do."

Simon stood up to leave, but Whitley wasn't quite finished.

"Oh, Mr. Lake, we have to carry out a thorough investigation into your financial affairs. I know we took away some bank statements and the like when we searched your property, but we need access to all your bank and building society accounts and all other investments."

"What for?"

"It's all just part of our enquiries."

"Trying to find out if I made cash withdrawals just before Kelly Taylor made one of her cash deposits?"

"We've got to check everything. Can you supply all the relevant details, please?"

"I'm an accountant, for Christ's sake – what do you think?"

"Thank you sir. Oh, and I'm afraid we will need the details of anything in your wife's name as well."

On the drive home Simon concluded that it would be a positive thing for him to prove there were no mysterious cash withdrawals that he couldn't account for. He rarely drew much cash out at all, preferring to pay for most things with cards. He usually kept no more than a couple of hundred pounds in cash in his wallet, unless they were going on holiday. Cash at holiday time was mostly converted into foreign currency or traveller's cheques.

He liked to pay for meals out with cash – not wanting to trust a waiter to take his card out of sight and wanting to minimise the waiting time involved when all he wanted to do was get out of a restaurant at the end of a meal. There were some relatively big bills occasionally for entertaining clients, but these were all settled on his company credit card. The three partners had an arrangement that the entertaining expenses of each of them were signed off by the other two.

He couldn't think of any significant cash withdrawal he had made that he couldn't explain. He would give the police all the documents they wanted.

Pippa was angry when he told her that Whitley wanted to know about all of her finances as well.

"Bloody cheek. So I'm a suspect as well, am I?"

"Well, I suppose they will suspect you of somehow aiding and abetting."

"What, aiding and abetting a murder?"

"No, darling, they will simply suspect that if I needed large sums of cash I might have done it through your account rather than mine, just for some added transparency."

"That's just bloody daft. You wouldn't need to be Einstein to figure that out!"

"No, but you know how they work. They have to plod down every avenue."

"I am getting really pissed off with all this. They're hounding my husband and now they're going to hound me. Neither of us have done anything."

She slammed the kitchen door and stomped up the stairs, shutting the bedroom door behind her.

When he went to the local shop the following morning, to scan the front pages of the papers, it was the headline in the Mail that hit him right in the eye.

'TORY MP's LINK WITH MURDERED KELLY'

His heart raced as he paid for the paper and hurried straight home to read it in private.

'Suffolk MP Mark Halsey was last night linked with the murdered Ipswich girl Kelly Taylor. A work colleague of Kelly's said she had seen her in Halsey's car in an NCP car park in Ipswich just days before she was murdered.

When the Mail tackled Halsey he initially declined to comment, but later stated that it must be a case of mistaken identity.

Mail reporter John Greaves was told by one of Kelly's fellow florists that she recognised Halsey because she had also seen him in the shop. She stated that she noticed his car, a large new Mercedes, outside the shop when he came in to order some flowers. She was certain it was the same car in which she later saw Kelly talking to Halsey in the Crown Street car park in Ipswich. Asked whether she had mentioned this to Kelly she confirmed that she had but said that Kelly had denied it. Apparently she had laughed it off, saying that he was way out of her league.

The tall, blonde haired Mark Halsey is a flamboyant character in the corridors of Westminster. Elected to parliament in the last general election, he has been identified as one of the Conservative party's rising stars. He founded Estyler Halmark, an Internet marketing business, in the late eighties and made his fortune when the company went public in 1999.

Halsey was reported to have left the company with a personal fortune of some forty million pounds to concentrate on his political ambitions.

Halsey and his wife Louisa, a well-known ex-model, live in Hanley Mansion near Ipswich. They have two daughters at private school.

To date the only other suspect known to have been questioned by the police in relation to the murder is Ipswich accountant Simon Lake, the man who found her dead body and reported it to the police.'

Simon read the piece over and over again. He turned on both the radio and TV hoping to find out more. They were following up the story at regular intervals on 'News 24' and used some archived film footage showing Halsey on a platform celebrating his election victory. With his long blonde hair, bespoke pinstripe suit and the beautiful Louisa on his arm, he cut an impressive figure.

They hadn't been able to speak to him but it was obvious that the world and his wife very much wanted to. Halsey was a very well-known figure in Suffolk – dynamic, controversial and very confident in his own abilities. Simon had been to a couple of business functions attended by Halsey but had never actually spoken to him. It was very hard to believe that Kelly Taylor had been mixing in his company, but she was a very attractive young girl.

If nothing else, it at least gave Simon the feeling that the pressure on him had just eased a little bit. Now that someone else was also under suspicion it would surely make the doubters wonder.

When Pippa came home from shopping, Simon couldn't wait to tell her the news.

She was sceptical. "I can't believe someone like him would get involved with the likes of Kelly."

"Well, somebody has been improving her bank balance and Halsey could certainly afford a few thousand."

"But what for? He wouldn't have to pay for sex."

"Maybe he'd find it exciting that way; the danger of getting caught and all that. Plenty of wealthy people choose to use hookers."

"Maybe, but he's not just rich, he's bloody gorgeous. Loads of women would throw themselves at him."

"Yes, but maybe he likes the lack of complications if he just pays for it. He wouldn't want anyone demanding an ongoing relationship, not when he's got the lovely Louisa."

Pippa wasn't convinced. "I just can't see it."

Simon was angry. "So I'm a more likely suspect, am I?"

"No, of course you're not. I don't mean that at all. I just can't see Halsey being a suspect, that's all. It just sounds to me like a bit of gossipy speculation that the tabloids have seized upon."

"Well, thanks for all your encouragement. Just when a piece of news comes through that shows someone else under a bit of suspicion."

"Look darling, it's early days. I know you didn't do it but I suspect Halsey didn't either. There will probably be all sorts of other more likely suspects coming to light. Just give it a bit of time."

"Oh, it's so easy to be nice and patient and rational when your neck isn't on the block."

Simon stormed off to his study again, slamming the door behind him. Pippa stood in the kitchen staring blankly at the wall.

He was so desperate for more news that he had both the TV and radio turned on while he also searched the net. Really it was just more of the same – everyone trying to talk to Halsey without any success. He found himself beseeching someone to say that Halsey had been arrested, but they didn't. He wanted to call Whitley, but knew he wouldn't get anything out of him.

It was the following day before he even saw a report saying that the police were believed to have questioned Mark Halsey. There was nothing else – no arrest and Halsey's office was stonewalling everyone with 'No Comment'. He was used to being in the media spotlight and he clearly wasn't going to do anything to stoke things up.

The media were trying to get comments from Halsey's office, the police, Conservative central office, Louisa Halsey and anybody else they could think of who had any link with him, however tenuous. The end result was still nothing.

TV news footage showed a media scrum outside 'Flowers For You' but the staff weren't letting them in. Simon was pleased to see two police cars parked right outside the shop – surely the girls were getting grilled over just what Kelly had been up to.

Over the next two days media interest in Mark Halsey quietened down. There was no news of an arrest, no film footage of Halsey being taken to a police station for questioning – nothing at all.

Simon could wait no longer. His frustration got the better of him and he phoned Whitley. "Hello, it's Simon Lake here."
A pause. "Yes, Mr. Lake, how can I help you?"
        "I'm trying to find out what's happening….with regard to Mark Halsey."
        "Well, I'm not really at liberty to divulge anything relating to our enquiries."
        "Oh come on, man, you know what I'm going through. Help me out, Whitley… please."
Another pause followed, longer this time. "Okay then, just between you and me, Mr. Halsey has been eliminated from our enquiries."
        "What? How?"
        "He has an alibi for that Sunday morning, a cast-iron alibi."
        "What is it?"
        "I shouldn't really be telling you this, but he was in bed with his wife. They were in London – they were having a lie-in at The Park Lane Hilton after a black-tie dinner the night before. They checked out at 1215."

"Well, is that the end of it? What if he'd paid someone else to eliminate her?"

"I'm sorry but you're getting carried away. I have to terminate this conversation."

"Is it because he's an MP, Whitley? Is it harder to hound the likes of him the way you hounded me?"

"Mr. Lake, I know you have been under a great deal of stress, but please try to keep things in perspective. Goodbye."

CHAPTER 10

Simon called John Black and talked it all through with him, but he was no help, saying they just had to bide their time and leave it to the police. He called Paul, his daughter Chloe and finally he also called Peter at the office. All of them could only offer the same advice – he should just sit tight and leave it to the police.

He couldn't and he wouldn't. The next morning he decided to buy flowers for Pippa, from 'Flowers For You'. He parked the car in a multi-storey, put on his golf jacket and pulled the hood up. The girl behind the counter eyed him warily. "Yes sir, can I help?"

"I'd like a bouquet for my wife, please – one of those hand-tied ones in a water bubble."

"Certainly sir, what flowers would you like in it?"

"Oh, you can choose. She likes autumn colours – reds, oranges, yellows. Something about thirty-five pounds, please."

"Do you want it delivered, sir?"

"No, I'd rather wait while you make it up, please."

"It will take about twenty minutes, do you have any other shopping to do?"

"No, it's okay. I'll wait."

The girl looked unsure, obviously disappointed that he was going to hang around. He looked vaguely familiar – she wondered if he was a reporter, on the snoop.

She showed him through to a seated area with albums neatly laid out on a low coffee table, showing examples of flower arrangements for weddings and funerals.

"You can wait through here. Help yourself to coffee – today's paper is over there."

He thanked her, helped himself to coffee from a machine and flicked through the pages of the Daily Mail.

After a few minutes another girl appeared, carrying some sort of floral display, which she placed on a pedestal in the corner. Simon hoped that she hadn't been warned by the other girl that there was some shifty-looking character in a hoodie waiting in there. He decided to try his luck.

"Hello there. It's a bit warmer this morning."

She smiled. "Yes, it was a bit parky first thing, though."

"I was so sorry to hear about your colleague. It must have been a dreadful shock for all of you."

Her eyes narrowed slightly. "Yes, it's been difficult. She wasn't just a colleague, she was a close friend."

"I saw the piece on the news about Mark Halsey – did Kelly really know him, do you think?"

She averted his gaze. "I don't know – but Kelly had a very hectic life. She knew lots of people."

"Was Halsey a customer here?"

"I'm really not sure. I'm sorry – I have to get on."

She hurried out and a minute or two later an older lady appeared, looking at him quizzically. "Your bouquet will be ready soon, sir."

"Thanks, there's no hurry."

"Would you like to write a card to go with your flowers?"

"No, it's okay. I'll be giving them to my wife personally."

"Are they for a special occasion?"

"No, I just need them for a bit of an apology."

She laughed. "What have you done – or shouldn't I ask?"

"Oh, it's nothing. I'm sure you've had a lot to put up with in here lately. Were you Kelly's boss?"

She searched his face. "Aren't you Simon Lake?"

"Yes, that's right. I found Kelly."

"I know – I've followed everything. I don't think there's been a newspaper I haven't read or a news report I haven't heard since all this started."

Simon was encouraged – she seemed prepared to talk.

"I've been through hell since I found her. It was such a dreadful shock but I never dreamt that the police would arrest me."

She was wary. "I suppose they've got to cover every angle."

"Yes and I just hope they are doing that with Mark Halsey."

She was watching him, sizing him up.

"I read in the papers that one of your girls said Mark Halsey was a customer here."

"Yes, that's true, but we've got thousands of customers."

"Did he buy flowers for his wife here?"

"I'm sorry – we never give that sort of information out."

"Well, that wouldn't be a secret, would it, a man buying flowers for his wife?"

She smiled warily. "All florist shops have to use their integrity to keep every transaction confidential. It's a bit of a nightmare at Valentine's with lots of people sending flowers with no accompanying message."

"So what happens if the recipient demands to know who their flowers are from?"

"We can't tell them. Not unless we have permission from the sender."

"What if it was the police who wanted to know?"

"That would be different. If it was a formal request from the police as part of an enquiry then I'd help them."

Simon tugged his hood down and looked at her earnestly. "I'm just trying to clear my name and help the police to find Kelly's killer. Until they do I'm living under a cloud, and quite frankly the stress and the worry of all this is horrendous."

She looked at him, assessing him. "I'm sure it must be awful for you, but I really can't tell you any more about one of our customers. I promise you I've been cooperating with the police, though. I've given them everything they've asked for and I'll carry on doing whatever they ask until they get to the bottom of this."

A girl came in with Simon's bouquet, handing it to him with a smile. He thanked them and headed back to the car, deep in thought. He felt he'd pushed things as far as he could without alienating the staff. The problem now was how to move things on further.

He was certain the girls in the shop knew a lot more than they were letting on, but getting it out of them wouldn't be easy. There was no reason why they should tell him any more – he wasn't the police. He knew that they might be spooked already, knowing that the prime suspect had actually been in to their shop, buying flowers and asking questions.

Pippa was pleased and surprised when he handed the flowers to her. "What are these for?"

"Oh, just an apology, I guess. I know I've been a pain lately but everything is really getting to me."

She smiled and kissed him on the cheek. "It's no wonder – you poor darling, you've been through hell."

"I just want something to happen. Halsey has an alibi that proves he couldn't have killed her but that's no reason for Whitley to give up on that front. If Kelly had something on him then he could have arranged for someone else to silence her for him."

She looked doubtful. "There's a big jump from somebody thinking they'd seen Kelly in his car, to him taking out a contract on her."

"It's one of the girls from the shop who is convinced it was her ... and she'd seen Halsey in the shop."

"Yes, but it's still a pretty tenuous link. She might have just flirted with him when he placed an order and he asked her out for a drink."

"But he's old enough to be her father, for heaven's sake."

"He's a well-known character though – good looking, rich and very much in the public eye. They say that power is the ultimate aphrodisiac. What a catch he'd be for a young girl like Kelly."

"I don't see it that way. You make it sound like a harmless little flirtation, but he's a married man. He might have paid Kelly for sex and she saw an opportunity to make some more money out of it. How do you think she makes all that extra cash?"

"I don't know, but you can be sure the police will be working on it."

"Will they? Or will they just assume all they have to do is find one little bit of real evidence that points the finger at me? I'm not convinced they're getting anywhere."

She gazed out at the garden. "Where did you buy my flowers?"
He looked down at his feet. "At 'Flowers For You'."
Pippa stared at him, eyes blazing. "You sod, all you wanted was a chance to poke around and quiz those girls."

"Well why not? All I did was make some small talk."

"You bloody idiot. They've probably already been on the phone to Whitley. You are not a policeman, Simon, you are a suspect. You need to just keep your head down but instead of that you're charging around making a bloody nuisance of yourself."

"So what do you want me to do, just sit around waiting for them to come and nail me? I need to put some pressure on them or else they'll take the easy way out. The prisons are full of people who've been stitched up by dodgy circumstantial evidence."

"Now you're just sounding paranoid."

"Well, funnily enough it's easy to be that way when you're under suspicion of murder. When you're a virtual prisoner in your own home. When you can't go to work or to the shops without everyone looking at you and wondering if you did it. Just try to understand how it feels."

With that he stomped up the stairs and took refuge in his study, while Pippa went outside and unceremoniously stuffed the flowers in the bin.

Instead of doing some work he sat at his computer and decided to Google Mark Halsey. There were so many hits it was hard to know where to start. Some related to his many business connections, some to his political life and some to a wide variety of society events. Simon started with Halsey's personal website.

There was a biopic of him, detailing milestones in his life from public school, all the way through university, his many business successes and his impressive election victory. There were pictures of the lovely Louisa and his daughters and of their palatial home, Hanley Mansion. Simon was surprised that his liking for self-publicity was quite so overt. He wondered that Halsey wasn't a bit more concerned to keep his private life outside of the public domain, for security reasons if for nothing else.

Simon browsed through a variety of sites to get some idea of the wider world of Mark Halsey. He obviously had stakes in a multitude of businesses and he was involved in all sorts of parliamentary committees and working groups.

Despite trawling through all sorts of sites that seemed to specialise in juicy celebrity gossip he was disappointed that he couldn't find a whiff of scandal anywhere. There were pictures of Halsey in the company of various beautiful women but in all of them Louisa was there at his side. Simon felt the resentment growing within him as he observed the wonderful world of The Right Honourable Mark Halsey MP.

He then turned his attention to Louisa Halsey. Google listed nearly as many hits for her as for her illustrious husband. Many of them related to her very successful career as a high-profile fashion model, but she was also linked with a number of charitable organisations.

As he stared out of the window, contemplating how he could find out more, an idea eventually came to him. It was a risky idea, possibly a very stupid idea, and he couldn't quite believe that he was even considering it, but he was desperate. He entered the words 'Detective Agency Ipswich' into the Google search window.

There were four hits – three aiming at corporate clients and one that looked as if its speciality was divorce. It was euphemistically called 'Watchers' and listed such services as surveillance and telephone bugging. Simon wondered if they protected clients against having their telephone bugged or if they actively bugged telephones on behalf of clients. Whichever it was, they looked like the sort of outfit Simon was looking for. The address listed was near the centre of Ipswich and he decided to give them a call.

A female voice answered on the first ring. They were either efficient or not busy. "Hello, Watchers."

"Hello there. I've seen your website and I think you might be able to help me."

"Yes sir, what sort of service do you require?"

"Er ... surveillance, I guess. I want someone watched."

"Would this be a marital situation, sir?"

"Um, not exactly but it's similar, I guess."

"Would you like to come in and talk your requirements through, sir? Then we can explain how we might be able to help and discuss the likely costs involved."

"Yes, I think that would be a good idea. How soon could you see me?"

"How about this afternoon, sir? Mr. Clarke could see you at, say, 2 pm."

"Okay, that would be fine."

"Right, sir. Can I have your name, please?"

"Yes, it's Lake, Mr. Lake."

"Okay, Mr. Lake, we'll expect you this afternoon."

Simon immediately began to have second thoughts. Whitley would be furious if he knew, Pippa would go nuts and Paul would think he'd completely lost his marbles. He had no idea quite what he even wanted from Watchers and absolutely no inkling of what it might cost. He decided there was nothing to be lost from at least talking things through with them.

When he found the address for Watchers he was tempted to turn around and give up on the whole idea there and then. There was a grubby side door with a badly painted sign, next to a tattoo parlour. The door opened on to a flight of uncarpeted stairs. As Simon stepped inside, a sensor made a beeping sound and he was aware of a CCTV camera looking down on him.

He climbed the stairs and a frosted glass door was opened by a brassy-looking woman who was wearing far too much make-up and what looked like her daughter's skirt. She showed him in to a bare little office where he was introduced to a scruffy-looking man behind a cheap desk.

The man offered his hand. "Hello there, I'm Jeff Clarke, how can I help you?"

Simon wasn't at all sure that he could help at all. Clarke looked like an aging student, probably about fortyish. His brown cord trousers hadn't seen an iron for a very long time and the tweed sports jacket was way past its best. Long dark curly hair and small metal-rimmed glasses completed a dishevelled academic look.

Simon sat on the wooden chair offered to him, wondering when it had last been dusted.

"To be honest, I don't know if you can help me. I want to find out more about someone who I think may have committed a serious crime."

Clarke's eyes narrowed. "Tell me more sir and then I'll see what we can do."

Simon decided he would have to be up front. "I wondered if you might recognise me, actually. My name is Simon Lake and I'm the man who found the dead body of Kelly Taylor."

Clarke nodded. "I thought you looked familiar. So I take it this is in relation to that case?"

"Yes, as you probably know I was arrested, questioned and then released without charge."

"But they still haven't arrested anyone else, have they?"

"No, and that's my problem. I don't think the police are getting anywhere. They had another suspect, the MP Mark Halsey, but they tell me he has a cast-iron alibi. Apparently he was staying in a hotel in London with his wife when I found Kelly's body."

Clarke nodded again. "So the police have given up chasing him?"

"Right – and in the meantime I'm a virtual prisoner in my own home. I've had graffiti daubed on my front door, I get hate mail and everyone treats me like a leper."

"Yes, I can see your problem but I don't know that you can really do anything about it until the police catch the real culprit."

"Correct – and they might never do that. I think they should still be pursuing the Halsey angle. He was seen with Kelly and yet he's denying it. She was depositing large sums of cash into her bank account yet nobody knows where the money came from."

"What do you think – was she on the game?"

"Maybe. She wasn't walking the streets but she could have been working as an escort girl. Maybe she was having an affair with Halsey and threatened to go public. He might have had her killed to keep her quiet."

"That's quite some assumption, Mr. Lake."

"Well, it's an assumption I think is worth checking out."

"What do you want me to do? How do you think I could help?"

"You could follow him, find out if he was seeing Kelly or anyone else. The girls in the florist's shop where she worked are obviously convinced that it was her that one of them saw in Halsey's car. They recognised him because he'd been a customer in the shop. You could find out who he was buying flowers for."

"Mr. Lake, you need to understand that this would be an expensive exercise with no guaranteed results. Halsey must live a jet-set life with lots of travel. If you want me to follow him you'll have to pay our daily fee plus all my expenses for travel, hotels and the like."

"What is the daily rate?"

"Its £250 and that's a lot to spend if I'm just killing time for days, sitting in corridors in Westminster or wherever just twiddling my thumbs."

"I've got to do something. Let's try this for a week initially and then take it from there. Find out what you can from the shop where Kelly worked. Check out everything he does, where he goes and who he talks to. I think he's got some sort of secret life and I want to know just what he was getting up to and what he's got to hide."

"You do realise that the police wouldn't be impressed if they knew you were doing this, Mr. Lake?"

"It's not illegal, is it?"

"No, its not actually illegal but it's very unusual, to say the least, for a suspect in a murder case to be doing the work of the police."

"Well the police aren't delivering the goods, so let's give it a try."

CHAPTER 11

Simon spent quite a while checking out Jeff Clarke's credentials. He had obviously been doing this sort of work for some time and he did have some impressive electronic equipment. While Simon was there he even demonstrated one gadget by using it to eavesdrop on two women they could see chatting on the pavement across the street. They were quite some distance away but Simon was amazed at just how clearly he could hear them chatting away about the new ranges of skirts and blouses in M&S.

The visual equipment was equally impressive – Simon had never seen zoom lenses like those Clarke possessed. He was left in no doubt that if Clarke was able to spot Mark Halsey doing anything at all that he shouldn't then he'd at least be able to record it.

He didn't want anyone else knowing that he was using Clarke's services, so he gave strict instructions about when and how to contact him. If Pippa or anyone else picked up the phone when he called, Clarke would simply pretend to be a client.

They agreed that he would start work the following day and Simon gave him a personal cheque as an advance payment that should cover the first five days.

As he headed back home, he agonised over just what he was starting. He knew everyone would say he was stupid, but they weren't in his situation. He had to get the cloak of suspicion lifted and this was the only way he could think of. He only wanted to find enough evidence to pass on to the police so that they could then take some positive action. If by some miracle the police made progress anyway, and caught the killer, then he figured he would simply call Clarke off, settle what he owed him and nobody would ever be any the wiser.

That evening Simon made a decision. He would go in to the office the following day and resume business as usual. He would get in at what had been his usual time, work a full day and then come back home at the usual time. He called Peter to tell him his plans and in the meantime he did some work on Charles Dalton's accounts to try to get back into the swing of things.

Pippa was pleased and relieved. She'd hated seeing him sitting around the house, unable to focus on anything for more than a few minutes. She had always admired his capacity for work and the way he could just keep going from early morning until late at night, snatch a few hours sleep and then get stuck into a new day. She prayed that life would settle down, but secretly she shared Simon's view that life couldn't be normal until Kelly's killer was caught.

Simon was the second person to arrive at the office – Peter was always the first in. He was reading the FT while making coffee in the kitchen, and he got an extra mug out of the cupboard for Simon.

"It's good to see you back, old man. Any news?"

"None at all. I haven't heard anything from the police for over a week. I don't think they're getting anywhere and I reckon they've already scaled down the manpower working on it."

Peter shook his head. "I wouldn't have thought so. The media interest has died down after Mark Halsey hit the headlines but I'd have thought the police would still be working overtime on it. Whitley knows his neck is on the block – there's more pressure on him than anyone."

"Anyone except me. To the police it's just a job but it's stopping me from living a normal life."

"It has to get easier with time. People will think that you were under so much scrutiny that they'd have been sure to nail you if you were the murderer."

"No, I don't see it that way. People won't feel comfortable around me until I'm proven innocent, and that can't happen until they catch the right person."

Peter shrugged. "So what do you plan to do today?"

"I'll have to do some work on Dalton's stuff. I've done a bit at home but I needed access to more of his files here. I'll do that tax report for Maynard Chalmers and catch up on other bits and pieces."

"Sounds good to me. I'd like nothing more than seeing you around the place just being your old self."

"I'll try, Peter. I'll try."

There were plenty of raised eyebrows when the troops arrived and they saw Simon. Some pretended to talk to him as if nothing had happened, some avoided him and some clearly didn't know how to react.

He worked straight through lunch, eating a cheese and ham sandwich that Jo had brought back in with her. She chatted easily with him about routine work stuff and asked if she could do anything. Simon said he needed someone to dig out some figures for him from Charles Dalton's files and he'd show them how to set up some spreadsheet formulae to process some tax options he'd figured out.

Jo came back half an hour later with a shy-looking girl trailing behind her.

"Simon, this is Sue Dempsey and she can help you with the Dalton work. Sue's with us on work experience – she's studying accounting at the college and she's pretty good on Excel."

He smiled and held out his hand. Sue reddened and looked at her feet as she gave him a limp handshake that felt like a wet kipper.

"Right then, Sue. Let me explain what I need you to do. I'll show you where the data is and then I'll set up the bare bones of the first worksheet. Once you're happy that you know what you're doing I'll leave you to get on with it."
She nodded and blushed again.

They set to work, but it was hard going. The total lack of eye contact was starting to irritate him. He was being as nice as he knew how but Sue was obviously as nervous as a kitten and slow to learn. He kept his patience and explained things over and over again. Around mid-afternoon she said she needed to use the bathroom and so he volunteered to get tea for both of them.

He brewed up and took the two mugs back in to his office. He waited and he waited but she didn't reappear. Eventually Jo came in and closed the door.

"I'm sorry, Simon. Jo's in the Ladies; she's not feeling too good."

"What's wrong with her?"

"I don't really know, maybe it's just the time of the month."

"Or maybe it's just me. A young girl shut up in an office with a suspected killer – it must be a difficult situation for her."

"No, you don't know what's wrong with her. Maybe it's just something and nothing."

"Well, tell her she can go home early and we'll try again in the morning. I don't want to frighten the kid, but I really do need to get some bloody work done."

Over dinner that night Pippa was keen to know how things had been in the office.

"A bit strained, I guess. Peter is fine, and Chris, and Jo. Most of the rest make a bit of small talk, some just seem to avoid me."

"Well, that's pretty good on your first full day back."

"I don't know. I think I terrified some work experience girl who's supposed to be helping me with Charles Dalton's work."

"It's bound to be hard for a young girl."

"Why?"

"Well it's obvious, darling. To be fair, she's in an awkward situation."

"What, working with a suspected murderer you mean?"

"You know what I mean."

"Yes, I know exactly what you mean. That's the problem. How the hell am I going to sort myself out if my wife doesn't believe in me?"

"That's not fair. I believe in you one hundred per cent but I can't force other people to believe in you. It's just human nature."

"It's persecution, that's what it is. I'm not blaming some work experience kid – I'm blaming Whitley and his motley crew for not bloody getting anywhere."

"Maybe she really isn't well. Maybe it's period pains or a bug or something. Just see what tomorrow brings."

"Yes and in the meantime you can just carry on with your cosy little life. Go and play golf with the girls, do some shopping, go for a drive, do the crossword, just pretend nothing's happened."

"You know I can't do that. I think about nothing other than this bloody situation from morning to night – I dream about it. I just wish you'd never ever had the daft idea to go trespassing on a cold Sunday morning."

"Yes, it's all my fault, isn't it – disrupting your comfortable life. It was terrible of that girl to get herself killed – you'd think she'd have known that it might inconvenience you. No consideration at all."

"I'm going to bed. I can't talk to you like this. Get yourself a stiff drink and a good night's sleep."

Simon didn't speak to her when he came up to bed – she was awake but pretended to be asleep. He got up early after a broken night's sleep and from under the covers she heard him drive away.

He tried to concentrate on working through his backlog of emails and wading through an in-tray full of bumf. After a while Jo brought him in a coffee.

"Morning Simon – thought you might need this."

"Thanks Jo. I need to crack on with Dalton's work. Is Sue in yet?"

She looked away. "I'm sorry – she's phoned in sick."

"Great, just what I bloody need. She's terrified of me, isn't she?"

"I don't know – she could just be genuinely ill."

"She isn't. You know that and I know that."

"Well, don't worry about it. I'll find someone else to help you."

"This time, try asking them first whether they object to working with a suspected killer."

She shook her head sadly and walked out.

Jo sent in Andy, one of the juniors. He was a big burly rugby player, with a ready smile, and if he had any worries about working with Simon then he certainly didn't show them. Simon felt they just might finally get some work done.

At lunchtime Jeff Clarke rang with his first progress report, but it wasn't encouraging.

"So tell me, what's he getting up to?"

"Well, Mr. Lake, it seems our man is a bit of a workaholic. I pretended to be a constituent of his, trying to find out when I could see him, and his secretary walked me through his diary for the next week."

"And what was in it?"

"Loads and loads of meetings – some in Westminster, some at his Ipswich office, some in various other places. He seems to do a lot of constituency work and he's on all sorts of committees and working parties."

"So where are you now?"

"In a corridor at the Commons. He's sitting in on some debate or other. He's due at a Commonwealth function at The Inn On The Park tonight."

"Well, keep tabs on him; find out who he sits next to. See if there are any women around him, other than the lovely Louisa."

"That might not be easy. The security is bound to be very tight – there are going to be several cabinet ministers there."

"Well, it's what I'm paying you for."

"Yes, Mr. Lake – I'll call you again as soon as I have any news."

Simon sat back in his chair, wondering just how much money he could afford to waste on a private eye wandering around London clocking up expenses. He worked late and arrived home to find a note from Pippa saying she was visiting one of her girl friends and his dinner was in the microwave. He fixed himself a large gin and tonic and half-heartedly watched a football match on Sky.

It was ten'o'clock when the phone rang.

"Hello, Mr. Lake."

"Hello, who's that?"

"Just somebody wanting to know when you're going to do the honourable thing and stop wasting the police's time."

"What do you mean?"

"Just own up, you murdering bastard. Everyone knows you did it. Do us all a favour and turn yourself in."
Simon put the phone down and then rang 1471. "You were called at 2158. The caller withheld their number."

He forgot about the meal in the microwave and got himself another G&T. When Pippa arrived home she knew right away that he was drunk and in a bad mood.

"Hello, darling, do you want to talk about it?"

"No I bloody don't."

"Do you want to know what sort of day I've had?"

"No I bloody don't. I don't care what sort of day you've had. I'm going to bed."

Pippa slept in the back bedroom and he was gone when she awoke in the morning. When the post arrived she recognised the envelope with the address written in crude block capitals and destroyed it before Simon could see it.

On the Thursday he had to visit Shadwell Marine, a boatyard on the banks of the Orwell, on the way out to Shotley. They had been clients for many years and wanted to talk about a new accounting system that would enable them to concentrate more on their core business.

John Shadwell had taken over the running of the family business after his father Stanley had died from cancer a few years back. Stan had been one of the old school – happy when working on the boats and grumpy whenever he had to spend any time on paperwork. When John took over they didn't have a computer, not even one single PC. He soon changed that and he had gradually transformed the business, but he knew there were limits to what be could do.

They now had four PCs for general office work and a sophisticated CAD system for the boat design work. They had proper systems for the sales ledger and purchase ledger, and as a result their cash flow had improved dramatically. Stan often used to hand-write an invoice for work months after it had been completed and then the customers would take an age to pay. John had changed all that. The year-end accounts were a different matter, though, and he was happy to let Chambers, Lake & Bradwell handle that for him. He wanted to improve their in-house accounting so it would make it easier, and less expensive, for Simon to check all their input and then complete their year-end.

John greeted Simon like the old friend he was. "Hello mate, how the hell are you?"
Simon grinned and shook his outstretched hand. "Not bad apart from all the hassle that goes with finding a dead body."
"Yes, obviously we heard all about it and I've been following all the news. Are the police getting anywhere?"
"No, I wish they were. They tell me they've still got lots of people working on it but I don't see any signs of them coming up with anything new."
"Incredible, isn't it? With only one decent road going to Shotley and such a small population out there you'd think they'd have come up with something. It must have all been such a strain for you - how is Pippa bearing up?"
"Oh, she's okay I guess. Stressed out like me."
John put his hand on Simon's arm. "Let me show you around. We've taken on some interesting new projects since I saw you last."

They walked around the boatyard, with John pointing out different boats and explaining what work they were doing on each of them. Then they went back to the office and over coffee they talked through the best way to tackle the new accounting project. When they'd finished agreeing a plan of action, Simon started to collect together all his paperwork.

John gazed out of the window at a small coaster heading up the river towards Ipswich. "Are the police checking out all the people who use the marina at Shotley?"

"I can only assume they are, why?"

"Well, I was out there a couple of months back seeing a potential customer who wanted me to quote for giving his boat a refit. We looked over the boat, agreed what needed doing and how much it would cost, and then we went into the bar at the marina for a drink."

Simon closed up his briefcase. "And?"

"Well, he was a pleasant sort and one drink led to another, how it does. There were quite a few people in there, drinking and eating bar snacks. Suddenly there was a real kerfuffle."

"What sort of kerfuffle?"

"Well, one of the girls who serves behind the bar slapped this bloke across the face."

"What did he do to deserve that?"

"She claimed he put his hand up her skirt when she walked past his table."

"What did he do?"

"Oh, he protested his innocence and left, looking really embarrassed, as you'd expect."

"Do you know who he was?"

"Well, I don't know his name but the customer I was with recognised him. Apparently he keeps an old yacht at the marina – he's always working on it and my customer thought that he lives on board a lot of the time."

Simon's eyes were out on stalks. "Well, that is really interesting. I'm going to contact the police – see if they've checked him out."

"Yes, it's worth a try. I'm not saying he's got anything to do with Kelly Taylor, but it's only a short walk from his boat to where you found her."

Simon pumped John's hand. "Thanks – any lead is worth pursuing. I'll get on to it and I'll write to you summarising what we've agreed on the accounting work."

CHAPTER 12

Simon was on the phone to Whitley as soon as he got back to the office. He explained what John Shadwell had told him but found Whitley evasive when he asked him if he knew about this yachtsman.

"We have been checking out lots of people, Mr. Lake."

"Yes, but have you checked this guy out?"

"I'm not sure, to be honest. I delegated the task of checking out everyone who uses the marina to one of my officers."

"So did you know about this incident? Did you know that somebody who could have been very close to the scene of the murder that morning had recently been involved in an unsavoury incident where allegedly he stuck his hand up a barmaid's skirt?"

"There's a big difference between someone allegedly groping a girl and murdering someone."

Simon was getting angry. "Yes, I do realise that, but both are incidents of assault on a girl even if they are far apart in terms of seriousness. It might indicate a pattern, though – a weirdo who preys on young girls."

"I will check it out, Mr. Lake. Thank you for bringing it to my attention."

"So what is happening, Whitley? Have you got any proper suspects? Just what the hell are you people actually doing?"

"We're continuing to work very hard, sir, and as soon as we have any news I will be in touch, I promise you."

Simon was seething and it only served to strengthen his conviction that he couldn't rely on Whitley and his troops to organise a piss-up in a brewery. His mood wasn't improved when Peter put his head around the door.

"I hate to mention it, Simon, but how are you getting on with Charles Dalton's work?"

"Why? Has he been chasing me up?"

"Yes, he tried to phone you and wasn't best pleased when he was told you were out seeing a client."

"Pompous sod – does he think he's the only client we've got?"

"No, but he knows he's the biggest and he's getting pushy about his year-end."

"Why? What's the problem? We don't have to file for ages and in the meantime I have been doing some work on his tax."

"Well, he wants to see you. I'm sorry, but I said you'd call in on him tomorrow to give him an update."

"Okay then, can't upset mister bloody big shot Dalton, can we?"

Peter grinned. "I'm sorry."

Dinner with Pippa that night was eaten in silence. He was consumed with his thoughts about the weirdo John had told him about. She had learnt that it was better to keep herself to herself at the moment. She hated his black moods and the way he was behaving so out of character.

She yearned for their life to revert to normal. They had always shared the day's experiences over dinner at night. She used to love the way that he could always make everything seem okay no matter what hassle the day might have thrown at them. They hardly ever argued, and on the very rare occasions they did have a tiff it was only over silly little things, and it was always sorted out before bedtime. Now life was very different, and she hated it.

After the meal Simon disappeared to his study to half-heartedly do some research on the Internet. He was looking for the best new deals for offshore accounts. He knew that Dalton would expect him to have some new ideas to help him accumulate yet more wealth.

When he arrived at Dalton's office he parked next to Charles' car – a Bentley Continental with a personalised number plate. Dalton liked people to know he had money and was shameless in the pursuit of it. Geraldine, his starchy secretary, ushered Simon in to the inner sanctum. Dalton's office was huge, with oak-panelled walls and bookcases full of impressive-looking tomes that Simon was sure he had never read.

Dalton was sitting behind an antique mahogany desk, leaning back in his huge leather reclining chair, legs stretched out, phone clamped to his ear. He wore his trademark Savile Row suit with a red silk tie. With his black hair slicked back and his face glowing with moisturiser he looked like the manager of an upmarket car dealership.

Simon couldn't avoid eavesdropping.

"Read your lease – a little problem with the bloody heating doesn't exonerate you from paying the rent."

He motioned Simon to sit down.

"Well, either you settle up by the end of this week or I'll have the bailiffs in."

He smiled at Simon and winked.

"You'll find out the hard way whether I'm serious or not. If you don't pay I promise you'll be out on your ear and I'll kill your crappy little business stone dead."

He slammed the phone down, still smiling. It was just routine everyday business for him. He knew how to get away with spending the absolute minimum on his many premises whilst maximising the rental income and frightening the hell out of anyone who crossed him.

Simon winced as Dalton shook his hand with the usual vice-like grip. Although he was now in his early fifties, he still worked out regularly in his gym at home and he liked everyone to know just how fit he was.

"Hello Simon, how are you? Terrible business about that girl."

"Hello Charles – yes it's been a tough time since I found her."

"Yes, it must be very difficult for you to concentrate on business, I guess?"

"Well it has been but I'm working pretty much as normal again now. I have been doing some work on your year-end and I think I've found a good new scheme in the Caymans that we should look at."

"Good stuff. Look Simon, to be honest I want my year-end sorted out ASAP. I don't want you sitting on all my paperwork indefinitely, there's stuff I need."

"Well, you can always let me know if there's anything specific that you need and I'll dig it out for you, but I've got boxes full of your paperwork at home that I need for the year-end work."

Dalton looked frustrated. "Well, don't take too long. I want everything back as soon as poss."

"I promise you are my top priority. I should have it all done and dusted in a couple of weeks."

"Are you sure? If there's a problem because of everything that's happened then I can always get someone else to handle things for me."

"No, really, Charles – I promise you I won't let you down. I was having to spend lots of time with the police and it was hard to work when the media were constantly parked outside the house, but it's all settled down now."

"So what exactly is happening? When are the boys in blue going to nail somebody?"

Simon raised his eyebrows. "God knows – I don't think they're making any progress at all, I wish they were."

"So do I, Simon. I want you back to your old self and keeping my bloody tax bills down. I reckon those sods at the

Inland Revenue must be bloody wallpapering their offices with all the money I give them."

Simon smiled. "Well, let me tell you about this new offshore account I've found. That should cheer you up."

The next hour was spent talking numbers and punching buttons on their calculators. Dalton was in the habit of tearing articles out of the Financial Times and the business sections of the Times and Telegraph and challenging Simon on why they shouldn't be using some new tax saving scheme that had taken his fancy. Simon had learnt that Dalton was easily taken in by eye-catching headlines but not so good at studying the small print.

Dalton had no real need to constantly amass more and more wealth, other then for the pleasure it gave him to accumulate it. He was a wealthy man who could never hope to spend more than a small fraction of his vast fortune, but he took great pleasure from counting it.

He doted on his wife Janet and had always been impressed by her pedigree. The daughter of Lord and Lady Templeman, she had been born in to money and Charles had always been proud of her links with the aristocracy. Although he had been to Eton his family had later fallen on hard times and he was largely a self-made man - but he had always envied Janet's natural style and her easy sophistication.

The next day Simon had every intention of getting stuck in to Dalton's work, but he was plunged into doom again as soon as he set foot outside the house. He hadn't bothered to put the car away the previous evening and had left it parked in the drive. There was an upturned tin of brake fluid sitting on the roof of the car and deep scratches all the way down both sides and across the bonnet. The brake fluid had already taken much of the paint off and it was obvious the entire car would have to be resprayed.

Simon retreated to his study and slumped in the chair. It was an hour before he could bring himself to call Peter to explain what had happened. He called the leasing company and they made arrangements to collect the car and provide him with a rental car as a temporary replacement. He also called Whitley to let him know that it was just the latest example of the hassle he was suffering because of the police's failure to do their job and clear his name.

He sat in the chair looking forlornly at the birds feeding in the garden, musing that he really would have to do something about all the patches of moss that were appearing on the lawn. The phone rang to rouse him.

"Hello Mr. Lake, it's Jeff Clarke here."

"Oh hi, Jeff, what's news?"

"Nothing much, I'm afraid. I'm still getting to know the corridors of Westminster and following him around from meeting to meeting. He went home last night and he's in Hanley today, holding one of his surgeries for constituents. I used to think that being an MP was a cushy number but it certainly isn't for this guy – he seems to work night and day."

"Do you know what he's doing the rest of the week?"

"Yes, I keep phoning his secretary pretending to be different people. I think I know almost as much as she does about what's in his diary. He's got a Chamber of Commerce meeting in Ipswich tomorrow morning, then he's doing an after-lunch speech for the Women's Institute. That's followed by a business meeting in Bury St. Edmunds and then a Rotary Club dinner in the evening. The man's always on the go – if he gets a spare five minutes he's on his laptop with his mobile to his ear. He even seems to have constituency stuff and business dinners filling up his weekend."

"He must have some time to himself. If he's so busy, how did he come to be sat in his car with Kelly Taylor?"

"I can't answer that, Mr. Lake but you have to accept it could simply have been mistaken identity."

"No, it wasn't – the girls in the shop are convinced it was him and I believe them. There's something we don't know about Mark Halsey and I'm relying on you to find out what it is."

"I'll do my best, but I can't promise anything. I have to warn you this is getting expensive though. Apart from my daily rate I'm clocking up a lot of expenses trailing around after him."

"I realise that, but so long as you get receipts and you can justify it all then I'll pay. It's not money that I want to be spending, but when you're in my situation you have to do what you have to do."

"Are you sure you're still under suspicion? It's easy to get things out of perspective."

"Look, my car was vandalised last night by some nutter – it needs a complete respray. That was all I needed to convince me that people won't stop persecuting me until this is resolved."

"I'm sorry to hear that, you really are going though the mill. I promise you that if Halsey puts a foot out of line I'll be on to him."

"Okay, keep at it and keep me posted."

Simon went back to staring out of the window. He mused that at least he had two possible suspects now. Surely something would happen soon that would shed some more light on to the whole sorry affair.

The doorbell rang – it was a man from Sterling Cowell to take his car away and leave him a replacement. Simon gave the loan car a very brief once-over and signed for it.

He decided to take himself off to Shotley for a pub lunch. He would visit both the pub and the marina bar and see if he could find out any more about the weirdo. He pulled on his golf jacket and the woolly hat that he usually only wore to football. He looked in the mirror – satisfied that he looked nothing like the man in the many pictures that had appeared in the media, he set off.

CHAPTER 13

Simon parked the car on the waterfront at Shotley, next to the King's Head. He figured he was in almost the same parking space as he had been on that fateful Sunday. He turned the radio off and sat there for a while, looking across the water to Felixstowe and Harwich.

There were four large container ships in Felixstowe docks. Huge cranes on the dockside lifted the containers on and off. He could see that the two largest ships were both from China and he wondered just what was in the thousands of containers they carried. He had always marvelled at the complicated logistics that must be involved in matching the correct containers to the right lorries, which then conveyed them on to all corners of the country. He wondered just what would be on the supermarket shelves around the country if the container industry should ever come to a halt.

When he'd been a boy seaman at Ganges Felixstowe had been a much quieter port. The development of it in to one of the world's largest container ports had all happened after he left. He remembered getting the ferry across one hot Sunday afternoon with a group of his messmates. They had walked along the front in their best number one uniforms eyeing up the girls.

As one cross-Channel ferry arrived in Harwich, another one left. He used to marvel at those ferries, wondering just what all those people did when they made their exciting journeys across the channel. He used to watch them and daydream about the day when he'd eventually join a real ship and visit foreign parts.

A variety of small boats came and went – some were out for a day's fishing and a few yachtsmen were taking advantage of the stiff breeze and defying the cold weather. He had often thought about buying a boat – just a small cabin cruiser. He could take Pippa along the Suffolk coast but she'd never been keen.

He tried to imagine Kelly parking her car here and wondered just who else had parked there on that Sunday morning. Had Kelly walked on to the Ganges site on her own and then met her killer? Or had they walked there together? For the thousandth time he wondered what on earth could have brought her here on that terrible day.

He entered the pub and was served by a cheerful plump woman. He ordered a glass of the red house wine and a roast beef sandwich on granary bread. The only other customers were all sat at the far end of the bar and so he decided to try chatting to her.

"It's cold out there today."
She smiled. "Yes, you want to stay in here by the fire."
"It must have been like this the day that girl was killed."
She looked bored with the subject. "Yes, it was."
"It seems to have pretty much dropped out of the news now."

"Yes but it hasn't stopped all our customers talking about it. Everyone's got an opinion but I don't think anyone's got a clue really."

"What do the locals think?"

"Depends on who you talk to. Some think it was somebody from Ipswich, some think it was a seaman off one of the boats, some think it was a local, some think it was that bloke who said he found the body."

Simon looked at his reflection in the mirror behind the bar and pulled his hat further down over his ears. "Do they think it might have been somebody from the marina?"

"Some do – they say there are people who stay overnight on their boats sometimes and they'd be only a short walk from where she was found."

"Does anyone have a particular sailor in mind?"

"Oh I've heard some talk about a strange guy who lives on his boat a lot of the time. There are rumours that he's a bit of a perv, so I suppose people are bound to suspect someone like that."

"Do you know his name?"

"No, I don't and I wouldn't want to accuse anyone."

She was looking wary now and Simon knew he'd asked as much as he could. His sandwich arrived and he sat down at a table, facing away from the bar.

As he gazed out of the window feeling the warmth of the log fire, he wondered if the weirdo might be on his boat right now. It was only a ten-minute walk along the waterfront to the marina and so he decided to go for a stroll.

The wind was biting – he pulled up the collar on his jacket and thrust his hands deep into his pockets. The water was choppy and the wind was blowing spume from the tops of the waves. He walked past the same gap in the railings that he had gone through before. Despite all that had happened, nothing seemed to have been done to prevent anyone from getting on to the Ganges site.

He decided to make a detour before checking out the marina. He walked up the hill to the main gate of Ganges. When he'd been a boy seaman the black iron gates had always been open. There was always somebody on duty, night and day, checking everyone who went in or out. Now the gates were closed and padlocked, with barbed wire along the top to stop anyone climbing over.

Through the gates he could see the 'DANGER – KEEP OUT' sign. Weeds grew high and thick across the parade ground and the roadway. He smiled as he remembered how little chance any weed had to flourish in the days when two thousand boys were kept busy keeping the whole place immaculate.

The mast was still there – he wondered if there was a preservation order on it. It was such a famous landmark; such a poignant reminder of times past.

He remembered the first time he'd had to climb it. They were instructed to climb to the devil's elbow, where the main rigging met a solid platform. This had been okay, but the next time they went up a PTI had urged them to climb outwards around the elbow and up to the next level. This had been very scary, and he had felt really vulnerable as he edged out around the platform with nothing but fresh air underneath him. A couple of his classmates had simply been unable to do it, but Simon remembered that he had forced himself – he was very scared but he was more worried about the potential loss of respect from the rest of the lads.

As the months went by, and he made more attempts, he got a little braver each time. He pushed himself to go higher, up to the cross-spar above the devil's elbow and then eventually up the very small ladder to the top cross-spar.

The next step was to shin up the very highest section to the button at the top – this took real courage and the boys found it to be the ultimate test of whether you had a head for heights. Simon never made it up that last section but he was satisfied that he had pushed himself to his personal limit; reaching the button was simply a step too far for him.

The button was a tiny circular platform, just about large enough to place two feet on. When standing on it there was only a lightning conductor to give any added support. This was a vertical rod projecting some eighteen inches above the button. On ceremonial occasions boys would climb the mast to the beat of a drum. The 'button boy' would climb to the very top and stand on the button with the lightning conductor gripped between his knees, before saluting.

It was a popular topic of discussion between the boys whether you had to be very brave, very stupid, or both to become a button boy. Certainly it commanded the respect of all their peers.

As he stood there braving the biting wind and staring up at the top of the mast, Simon remembered Robin Russell. He had been a small quiet lad who kept himself very much to himself. One hot Sunday afternoon Simon had seen Robin walk out of the mess with a paperback book in his hand. To the utter astonishment of every boy in Ganges he was later seen sitting on the button, casually reading his book while he soaked up the sunshine. From that day onwards Robin Russell had everyone's total respect.

He mused that Ganges had a way of testing the limits of each boy and letting you know where you stood in the pecking order. He looked at the remains of the CMG – the Central Messing Galley – to the left of the main gate. It was now completely surrounded by nettles and weeds, and many of the windows were broken. This had been where they all ate three meals a day, each and every day. It was a huge canteen with lots of long tables and the queue of hundreds of hungry boys would stretch right around the outside.

He remembered one boy, John Cox, who was much bigger than the rest of them – well over six foot, even when just fifteen years old. He was cocky when no instructors were around and liked to throw his considerable weight around. One day when Simon was about two hundredth in the line for dinner Cox was jumping the queue as per usual until one lad stuck his foot out. Cox had been busy looking out for any instructors and didn't see the outstretched foot; he tripped over it and fell headlong on the floor.

Cox scrabbled to his feet, red-faced with fury, searching for the boy who had dared to challenge him. Everyone had expected the lad to run for it but he did the opposite. He was a good six inches shorter than Cox but he stepped up to him with a smile on his face and clearly no intention of backing down. It was the Ganges version of High Noon – all the boys held their breath. Cox looked at the smiling face and when he detected no sign of fear he meekly walked back to the end of the queue. He was never seen to queue-jump again – Ganges did that sort of thing to bullies.

It was always said that large helpings of bromide were poured in to the huge tea urns in the CMG to suppress the sexual urges of all those young boys. Simon had always wondered whether this was apocryphal.

After a time they were allowed out of Ganges for shore leave on a Sunday. Many of them would board buses for the journey in to Ipswich, where they would chat up the local girls. Some of the girls were known to go only with Ganges boys and they were laughingly referred to as seaweed. Simon could remember having a kiss and a cuddle in a back street near the bus station, but he didn't really recall any strong sexual urges. Maybe it was true about the bromide.

Simon smiled at how naïve they all were as young boys. He remembered them all forming up one day for the instructor to allocate jobs to them. He had smiled and asked if any of them liked films. Stupidly Simon had raised his hand, only to be handed a broom and told to sweep out the cinema. It was a very large cinema and it needed a lot of sweeping – he knew the instructor would inspect his handiwork. You soon learned not to volunteer.

He sighed and trudged back down the hill, past the pub and along the waterfront. It was an impressive and well-equipped marina with lots of facilities. There were hundreds of berths, a dockside toilet block, a restaurant and bar, a chandlery, a laundry and an extensive boat repair yard with a hoist and crane.

Adjacent to the marina was the HMS Ganges museum, where he'd spent several pleasant Sunday afternoons browsing through photographs and artefacts and reminiscing about the old days. A sign in the window said it wouldn't be open until April. He decided to check out the bar.

There were just half-a-dozen people dotted around the bar area. Simon positioned himself well away from them at the far end of the bar and ordered another glass of wine from the young barmaid. He wondered if she was the one who'd felt the unwanted hand up her skirt and decided to see what he could find out.

"Not many people around today."

"No, not surprising at this time of year."

"I guess there's hardly any sailors around in the middle of winter?"

"Oh there's always some. It amazes me that people want to go sailing out there in the freezing cold, but some do and there's always people working on their boats all the year round."

"Do they live on their boats?"

"Very few do in the winter. In the summer plenty of people will spend the weekend on their boat. They can use the facilities and eat and drink in here if they want to get off their boat."

"But they don't do that in winter?"

"Not really, maybe for the odd night."

"I'd heard there was one guy who spent a lot of time on his boat, all year round."

Her eyes narrowed. "That would be Joe Clemence."

"Oh right, what sort of boat has he got that he can stay on board in this sort of weather?"

Now she was uncomfortable. "I really don't know. Excuse me, I've got to collect glasses."

Simon watched her collect up a few dirty glasses and then disappear through a side door into the kitchen area. Shortly afterwards he became aware of another girl looking at him through the window in the kitchen door. He finished his drink and went back out into the cold.

There was a walkway across the lock that formed the entrance to the marina. Simon crossed this and followed the path that led all the way around the berthing area. There were hundreds of boats moored in neat lines and he looked for signs of life on any of them.

He spotted a couple sitting at a table inside the cabin of a smart motor cruiser and one brave soul halfway up the mast of a large Bermuda-rigged yacht. He walked across the lock path, around the far end of the marina and then back on to the side that bordered the Ganges site.

As he passed a small sloop, he noticed a man on his knees in the hull scraping down the paintwork on the gunwale. He was young, probably in his late twenties, and good looking. Simon was convinced that he couldn't be Joe Clemence.

He stopped on the quayside, looking down. "You're brave, doing that in this weather."

The man looked up and grinned. "It's got to be done. Once the good weather arrives I don't want to be doing maintenance, I want to be out there with the sail up."

Simon smiled. "Good for you. Actually, you might be able to help me. I'm looking for Joe Clemence; he keeps his boat here but I don't know which one it is."

The smile was gone. "He's got Young Gazelle, a yacht, blue and white hull. It's about fifty yards further along but I don't think he's there today. Excuse me."

He moved into the small cabin of his boat and busied himself coiling up a rope. Clearly the conversation was over.

He soon found Young Gazelle, a worn-looking ketch that looked in need of a new paint job. The cabin was closed up and it was obvious there was nobody on board. Simon spent a few minutes taking a good look at it and then resumed his walk back toward the car. He resolved to find out more about Joe Clemence.

When he got back home the phone was ringing.

"Hello, Simon, it's Peter. Did you get the replacement car okay?"

"Yes thanks. I've just been out in it."

"Are you coming in today?"

"Er, no. I think I'll do some work at home."

"Look, old man, I don't want to hassle you but don't you think it's better for you to be in here getting on with business as usual?"

"Probably, but I've got sidetracked onto something else that I need to follow up."

"What do you mean?"

"Another lead came up when I went to see John Shadwell at the boatyard."

"What do you mean, another lead?"

"He heard about some weird guy who's been living on his boat at the marina in Shotley. There was an incident involving a young barmaid."

He could sense the frustration at Peter's end.

"Look Simon, for heaven's sake, you've got to just pass anything like that on to the police and let them get on with it."

"I would if I thought I could trust them to make the most of any new leads, but I can't."

"So what have you been doing? Where have you been?"

"Just out to Shotley to have a look around."

He heard the exhalation of breath from Peter.

"Bloody hell, that's nuts. That is absolutely stupid. You are going to get yourself in to real trouble playing the amateur detective."

"What, more trouble than I'm in already?"

"You're not in trouble. You found a body, you've been questioned and you were released."

"And most of the people in Ipswich look at me like I'm the Yorkshire Ripper. I've had threatening letters, phone calls and emails. My house and my car have been vandalised. Does all that sound like someone who's not in any trouble?"

Peter backed off. "Okay, I'm sorry. I only want to help but I do think the best thing is for you to try to live as normal a life as possible."

"You want me to do what's best for the firm, but sometimes you have to look after yourself. I'll come back in when I'm good and ready, maybe later in the week."

Simon put the phone down and stared blankly out of the study window, watching a squirrel hanging from the bird feeder. He'd never fallen out with Peter over anything before. Occasionally they'd had some heated discussions over work issues, but that was just part and parcel of everyday life in a busy office. He had never had anyone question his work ethic, though. He'd worked all hours, seven days a week, when they were building up the firm and he still worked probably sixty hours plus every week.

He heard the front door open – it was Pippa, back from the golf club. She came up the stairs and put her head around the door.

"Hello darling, how are you?"

"Oh, so-so, I guess. I've got a replacement car so at least I'm mobile again."

"Have you been to the office?"

"No, I've been out for a walk and a pub lunch."

"Where did you go?"

"Shotley."

Her eyes narrowed. "Why Shotley?"

"Just having a nose around. I found the boat that belongs to the pervy guy John Shadwell told me about."

She looked at him nervously. "You didn't see him, did you?"

"No, the boat was all closed up."

"And what would you have done if he'd been there?"

"I don't know. I just wanted to find out more about him."

"I really don't like this. The police would be furious with you if they knew that you were poking around, doing your own investigating."

"Yes, I guess they would."

She put her hand on his arm. "Please stop torturing yourself. This whole business is starting to affect your thinking. You're known as a level-headed and successful professional man. You're also a nice guy and that's the person I married. I don't like seeing you poking around trying to solve a major crime that the police are working on."

"You've told me all that before, but they're making absolutely no bloody progress whatsoever."

"You don't know that. They could be just about to arrest someone for all you know."

Simon made a snorting sound. "Some bloody hope."

"Well, I don't know what to suggest, but quite frankly this is all really getting to me."

"Then thank your lucky stars you aren't a suspect. If you were then you'd really know what stress is. It's best that you just leave me alone and let me try to handle things my way."

She put her arm around him. "Just don't get yourself into trouble, I beg you."

The weekend was brightened up for Simon by the visit of daughter Chloe, her husband Jason and their two daughters, Sam and Becky. They all spent Saturday afternoon together in the park. The children played on the swings and fed the ducks. Simon even played hide and seek with the girls, running in and out of the trees. Pippa watched her husband with a mixture of relief and delight as she squeezed Chloe's hand tightly.

"That's the first time I've seen your Dad laugh since he found that girl."

"Oh Mum, I've felt so awful not being able to come down and see you both. How is he bearing up?"

"Not good, to be honest. I've never seen him so low. He's had hate mail, his car was vandalised and we had graffiti daubed on the front door. What worries me most is that he thinks the police have got it in for him and that they aren't pursuing anyone else."

"You don't believe that, do you?"

"No, but your Dad certainly does; he seems to have lost his grip on reality."

Chloe took the opportunity to walk with her Dad, out of earshot of the others. She put her arm through his. "You do know that we all believe in you, Dad, don't you?"

He smiled. "Yes, and maybe one day everyone else will, but in the meantime life's not too good, to be honest."

"Be strong, Dad, be strong. Mum just wants to help you."

"I know she does, but sometimes it's better if she just lets me do my own thing."

"You've always been a couple – doing things together, supporting each other."

"I've never been a murder suspect before."

CHAPTER 14

At dinner that night Pippa served up a hotpot, Simon poured them all large glasses of Shiraz and Chloe lit candles. They talked until past midnight, the alcohol helping to push away Simon's darkest thoughts.

They took the girls to church in the morning and then lunched in one of their favourite restaurants in Woodbridge. They all ate too much and then attempted to walk it off afterwards by following the river path as far as they could. Late in the afternoon they returned home and Chloe and Jason packed, ready for their return to London.

Saying goodbye took ages, as the girls hunted for lost toys and chased around the house while Chloe and Jason loaded up the car. Simon and Pippa waved until the car was out of sight, but as soon as they were gone Simon felt the despair returning. He retreated to his study again, staring blankly out of the window. He wondered if his children would ever have to visit him in prison.

Pippa felt low too. It had been so lovely to see Chloe and the girls, but now the feeling of anticlimax really hit her hard. Unbeknown to Simon she had stopped going to the golf club. She was still putting on her golfing trousers and putting her spiked golf shoes and golf-balls in the car but then she would take herself off for a drive and a walk in the park. The girls in her usual foursome were nice enough but she just couldn't handle the furtive glances from all the other members. She knew they were all whispering behind her back, speculating on what was going on and probably commenting about how on earth she could be out playing golf after what had happened to her husband.

She also felt insecure, partly because of how distant Simon had become, but also physically insecure because of the vandalism. She hated the idea that anyone would ever encroach upon their privacy but now she felt that their own home had been desecrated.

Jeff Clarke called with another update. Mark Halsey had evidently been a paragon of virtue throughout the weekend. He had attended a fund-raising lunch on the Saturday in aid of cancer relief and then attended Ipswich's home match against Stoke before appearing as guest of honour at another fund-raiser in the evening.

On Sunday he had spent the whole day with his family. In the morning he had taken Louisa and the girls to church before they lunched back at Hanley Mansion. Then in the afternoon they all drove up the coast and took a long walk along the beach from Aldeburgh to Thorpeness and back again. Clarke said he'd never had so much fresh air in one weekend.

He asked Simon if he was really sure he wanted him to follow Halsey back to Westminster again.

"Yes I do; just remember what the girls saw. He's hiding something. He might be squeaky clean most of the time but you tell me what he was doing with Kelly."

"Okay, Mr. Lake, but I hope you've got deep pockets. My bill just keeps getting longer, I'm afraid."

"Just let me worry about that. You keep at it and make absolutely bloody sure you don't miss a trick. If he even drops a sweet wrapper then I want to know about it."

Gazing out of the study window he figured that he couldn't afford to keep using Clarke indefinitely. He would have to shuffle some money around so that Pippa didn't get wind of what he was up to. He used the online banking system to move five thousand from his personal E-savings account into his current account.

The police check on his financial affairs hadn't thrown up anything he couldn't answer. There wasn't anything to find – he had done very well from the firm in recent years and had no reason to do anything devious. He had used some offshore accounts and transferred money into some trust funds. Mostly this was with the specific intention of minimising any future inheritance tax liability, but it was all perfectly legal and above board.

He avoided the office again on Monday, opting instead to take himself off to Shotley once more. He parked his car at the marina and then walked along the path to where Young Gazelle was moored. It looked just the same as it had before the weekend, and there was no sign that Joe Clemence had been on board.

He had a glass of wine and a sandwich in the marina bar and was walking back towards the car when he saw a man unloading some tins of paint and a large rucksack from a battered old Volvo estate. Simon had a hunch; he pretended to just be out for a stroll around the boats. The man was scruffily dressed in jeans, a big woolly sweater, anorak and wellies. His hair hadn't seen a comb for a while and his greying beard needed a trim.

He watched the man lock his car and lug his load towards the shore side of the marina. His heart raced as he watched him climb on board Young Gazelle and unlock the door to the small cabin. He wasn't surprised that his hunch proved correct – the man definitely fitted the mental picture he had already formed of him.

He walked idly past the yacht to the very end of the line of boats, watching what was happening and figuring out what he might say. He turned and retraced his steps, feeling nervous as he approached Clemence's yacht again. He was busy stowing the tins of paint in a locker in the stern of the boat. Simon stopped and smiled, Clemence looked up, enquiringly.

"Not taking her out today, are you?"

"No bloody fear. Need to do some work on her."

"I'm wondering whether to move my boat here."

"What have you got?"

Simon lied. "Oh, just a small motor cruiser. I usually keep it at Levington."

The man nodded and started undoing the straps on his rucksack. Simon struggled to think of something to keep the conversation going. "Do you use the marina much in the winter?"

"Yeah, the boat's here all through the winter."

"But what about you? Do you stay here at all?"

"Sometimes, there's nothing to stop you."

"I heard that girl was murdered somewhere near here. Funny place for a young girl to be walking on a cold morning."

Clemence looked wary. "I only know what I read in the paper and saw on the telly."

"You weren't on your boat when it happened?"

"You're asking a lot of questions. Are you police?"

"No, just curious, that's all."

"Well, I need to unpack and sort some stuff out."

With that Clemence entered the cabin and closed the door behind him.

Simon drove straight home and called Jeff Clarke on his mobile.

"Jeff, I've got an extra job I'd like you to do."

"Sure, what is it?"

"I want you to find out all you can on a guy by the name of Joe Clemence. He keeps a boat at Shotley marina and the local gossip is that he's a bit of a perv. Sometimes he sleeps overnight on his boat and I'd love to find out if he did that the night before Kelly died."

"Okay, I'll do what I can."

"What's Halsey up to?"

"Right now he's sitting in the debating chamber and he's got meetings lined up all afternoon. I've been chatting to one of his researchers who's worked for him for the past couple of years."

"What does he have to say about him?"

"Only good stuff, I'm afraid. He told me he was a hard taskmaster, always on the go, very busy."

"He didn't volunteer anything on his personal life?"

"No, I asked him various questions in a roundabout way, but as far as this guy is concerned he's a loving husband and a devoted father. No dirt, I'm afraid."

"Did you mention anything about Kelly Taylor?"

"Yes, I said I'd seen the reports in the press about him being seen with her."

"What was his reaction?"

"Just that it had to be mistaken identity, someone trying to stir things up to make a story."

"Okay Jeff, keep at it and call me when you've got anything on Joe Clemence."

He really was starting to wonder how long he could afford Jeff Clarke nosing around and not coming up with anything. It wasn't his fault if Halsey wasn't doing anything that he shouldn't. All he could do was hope and pray that something would happen soon.

He wondered long and hard about whether he could be doing anything else. He would have loved to quiz the girls in the shop some more, but he knew they'd be wary of him now. In any case it was very unlikely that they'd tell him anything they hadn't already told the police. He even wondered about making contact with Kelly's family, but figured the same would apply to them and they might even be hostile towards him. Maybe he'd get Jeff to approach them.

Simon knew that really he should be getting on with life as normal and going into the office, but he was feeling more and more paranoid. He found it hard to do anything in the office when everyone was so uneasy just being around him. In the past he'd always been a stickler about clearing his in-basket and keeping bang up to date with everything. Now it was different – every time he tried doing some work at home his mind would wander back to the same old subject and he couldn't apply his mind to anything else. He thought continuously about Mark Halsey and Joe Clemence and why there was no news from the police.

He wandered idly around the garden. The mild winter meant that the bulbs were progressing fast; the snowdrops were out and soon there would be crocuses and even daffodils. The climate change doomsayers would be holding this up as absolute proof of global warming. He wondered if Whitley and his boys might possibly make any progress this side of the next ice age.

He eventually decided that a new approach was called for and headed back inside to the warmth of the study. He dug out some of the old newspapers that had carried stories of his arrest and his subsequent questioning by the police. Some of the more lurid tabloid reports made for very difficult reading. The broadsheets had been mostly factual and fairly accurate, but if anything they had lacked a lot of the insight of the tabloid Rottweilers.

He studied them all and browsed their websites, and finally came to a decision. The most accurate and sympathetic reporting had been from John Greaves of the Mail. Simon

Googled his name and found masses of stuff about him on the net.

As well as reporting for the Mail, Greaves did freelance work for all sorts of other papers and magazines. He had also written several books on crime and injustice that had been widely acclaimed by a number of reviewers on Amazon. Simon decided to call him, but tracking him down was not easy and he had to leave a message.

He didn't have to wait long for Greaves to call back.

"Hello Mr. Lake, it's John Greaves. I understand you wanted to speak to me."

"Yes that's right. Do you remember who I am?"

"Yes, I most certainly do. How can I help?"

"I need to talk to the press, but not just to anyone. I picked your name as you were one of the few to accurately report what happened to me when I was arrested and then subsequently released."

"I would love to have the chance to talk to you, Mr. Lake. Do you want to talk now or should we meet?"

"I want you to visit me at my home. Just you – no photographer or anyone else."

"Certainly sir." He hesitated. "Were you looking for any sort of a fee for giving your side of the story?"

"No, I don't want to make anything out of this. I just want to clear my name. I've been pilloried by most of the media and I can't get on with my life. I get hate mail, my house and car have been vandalised and I've become a leper in the local community. I don't hear anything from the police and this whole enquiry just seems to have got completely bogged down. I think it's about time I spoke out and the public knew my side of things."

"I understand that completely and I'd love the chance to put your side of the story to our readers. When can I see you?"

138

"As soon as you like. I'm at home now and so the sooner the better as far as I'm concerned."

"I'll come right away. I'm in London now and so I'll be with you in a couple of hours."

He knew Pippa wouldn't approve and nor would John Black or Whitley – but sod it, enough was enough.

CHAPTER 15

John Greaves was true to his word – he was at the house in just under two hours. Simon mused that he probably couldn't believe his luck at being invited to talk to the prime suspect in the Kelly Taylor murder case.

Simon sat him down at the table in the dinette and made two mugs of coffee.

"So, Mr. Lake, what exactly do you want to tell our readers?"

"I want them to understand what it's like to find a body, to attempt resuscitation and then to find out that you are the one under suspicion as the killer."

Greaves nodded, scribbling furiously in his notebook. Simon was surprised he didn't use a tape recorder.

"I don't think the police are making much progress, if any, and people need the killer to be caught before they can come to terms with what's happened and start to rebuild their lives. I feel so sorry for Kelly's family and friends – not knowing must be so painful for them."

"And for yourself – how do you feel?"

"Awful. I've had graffiti painted on my front door, paint stripper poured over my car, I get hate mail, threats over the Internet and yet I've done absolutely nothing wrong. So quite frankly, yes, I do feel sorry for myself too, and for my family and friends."

"What makes you think the police aren't making any progress?"

"Because I don't hear anything from them. There is nothing new in the papers and it's as if the trail has just gone cold."

"So what more do you think the police should be doing?"

"Working harder on what few leads they do have and finding some new leads."

"But maybe it's not easy to do that. Maybe the killer covered his tracks so well that the police have nothing more to work on."

"Well, they could find out what Kelly was doing in an MP's car for a start."

"I understood they had followed that up and Mark Halsey was able to prove he was staying in a London hotel with his wife."

"Maybe he was, but that still doesn't prove that he wasn't sitting in his car with Kelly just weeks before her death."

"Perhaps the florist got the wrong person?"

"No, I don't think so, she was certain alright."

Greaves quizzed Simon for another couple of hours before they were finally through. He was eager to call the office and get the story filed in time for the following day's first issue. Simon shook his hand and held on to it as he looked into Greave's eyes. "Promise me that you'll write a factual piece telling it as I've told you."

Greaves held his gaze. "Yes, I honestly do promise you that I will. I really do appreciate you giving me this opportunity to put your point of view. I'd like to keep in touch with you and talk to you some more as things develop. I know that you will only give me that chance if I'm absolutely straight with you and report it as it is."

Simon was thankful that Greaves had left before Pippa returned home. That night he would tell her what he had done but he wouldn't let her talk him out of going public.

He was up early the following day, ready to go the paper shop. He'd seen a preview of the story when he turned on the TV to look at the early news. In the 'what the papers say' section they showed the front page of the Mail with a banner headline 'Murder Suspect Slates Police.' When he first saw that he shuddered, but then he figured that was exactly what he was doing and it was what he needed to do.

Simon bought the Mail, the Telegraph and the local paper at the shop and was back home before Pippa had even woken up. He spread the Mail out on the dinette table and read every word, several times.

It was a bit of a shock to see it all in print, but it was accurate. Greaves had reported just what he had told him and had put little in the way of interpretation on it. It did make it sound as if Simon was really having a go at the police but then he was; he meant to.

The phone rang. It was John Black. "Bloody hell, Simon – I thought we agreed you would talk to me before doing anything rash."

"I'm sorry but it just got to me. I had to do something."

"But why? You'll only antagonise the police and this stirs it all up again, just when the story was going quiet."

"Well, maybe this will stir them into some action."

"Let me know if you hear from Whitley, Simon, and please don't do anything else like this before you've talked to me."

"I haven't done anything illegal. All I've said is that in my opinion the police are dragging their feet and that is indeed my honest opinion."

The kitchen door opened and Pippa appeared in her dressing gown. She sat down and read the paper without uttering a word and then looked at him. "So you think this is going to help, do you?"

"It can't do any harm."

"Of course it bloody can. It was all dying down and now you have to whip it all up again and get us back in the news. Why the hell couldn't you talk it through with me first, get a second opinion? I am your wife, you know – we used to be able to talk."

"I'm sorry but I need to do this my way. Nobody has been helping me and so I figured I'd have to start helping myself."

"Oh, so I haven't been helping you, then?"

"No, not really. I don't even know where you are half the time."

She shook her head sadly and went upstairs to get dressed.

The phone rang again. It was Jeff Clarke.

"Hello Mr. Lake, I've got some news for you."

"Halsey or Clemence?"

"Joe Clemence. I've done some checks and I thought you'd want to know that he's on the sex offenders' register."

"Bingo! What for exactly?"

"Indecent assault on a young girl in Barnsley in 2003. He did eighteen months inside for it."

"Anything else on him?"

"No, so far that's all I know."

"Well done, Jeff. I'm going to let DI Whitley know about it right away."

It took a while to get hold of Whitley as he was in court, but eventually Simon tracked him down.

"Ah, Mr. Lake, I've been reading about you in today's paper. I had hoped you'd keep your head down and let us get on with our work."

"I would if I thought you were getting somewhere, but I reckon I can find out more than you lot."

"And what exactly does that mean, sir?"

"Do you know someone by the name of Joe Clemence?"

"Yes, we do. He keeps a boat at the marina at Shotley."
This took Simon by surprise. "Okay, but do you know he's on the sex offenders' register?"

"Yes we do, and as a result we've interviewed him at some length and made various other enquiries."

"So is he a suspect?"

"He was but now he isn't."

"Why not?"

"Because Mr. Clemence can account for his whereabouts on the day Kelly Taylor was murdered."

"And you believe him?"

"Yes we do, because he's been able to prove beyond any doubt that he was in Amsterdam all of that weekend."

"Oh, I see."

"Was there anything else sir?"

"Well, you tell me. Have you got any other suspects?"

"We are working on a number of different lines of enquiry. It's a shame if you can't believe that but it is true. I know how important it is for you that the killer is found, and I can only give you my word that we are continuing to work very hard on this case."

Simon put the phone down. He felt utterly deflated. He wondered whether to go for a walk or a drive to try to clear his head and figure out what to do next. Instead he headed for the drinks cupboard.

The gin only served to make him feel even more depressed, but he drained the glass and refilled it, pouring in more gin than tonic. The alcohol was really taking effect by the time Pippa walked in.

"Where've you been?"

"Hello, darling."

"Hello – I said where've you been?"

"To see Mandy Roberts, for tea and a natter."

"Oh very cosy, telling her about your loony husband, I suppose?"

"She saw the Mail; she sympathises."

"But nothing more to offer than tea and sympathy?"

"What can people do, Simon? We've got lots of friends who'd love to help if they could, but what the hell can anyone do?"

"The perv on the boat at Shotley has got an alibi."

"How do you know that? Have you been talking to the police?"

"Yes, Whitley says the guy can prove he was in Amsterdam all weekend."

Pippa put her arm around his shoulder. "So that's a dead end."

"Yes, so I reckon it has to be Halsey."

"But he's got an alibi too."

"Yes, but people like him get someone else to do their dirty work for them."

"All you've got on him is that one of the florists thinks that they once saw Kelly in his car."

He mumbled something Pippa couldn't hear and took refuge in his study again.

He'd received Jeff Clarke's invoice for his first week's work and it was a bit of a shock. Apart from five days work at £250 per day, the Saturday and Sunday had each been charged at £375 on a time-and-a-half basis. Then there was nearly £1500 worth of expenses for hotels, meals, car mileage, rail fares and taxis. With VAT the total was well over four grand.

With Clarke now well in to the second week, he knew a similar bill would soon be on its way. Sitting at his PC he got in to the online banking system and moved some more funds across from his E-savings account to his personal account. The E-savings account was now down to just over three thousand pounds and he needed more readies.

He had other funds in term deposit accounts but they all required at least three months notice of withdrawal to avoid losing out on the interest. Simon figured that Jeff was bound to come up with something soon, and then his fees would be money well spent.

He looked at the piled-up boxes of Charles Dalton's paperwork and decided that tomorrow he really would have to get some work done.

First thing the following morning his hunch proved right. Jeff Clarke was on the phone. "Sorry to call so early, Mr. Lake but I know you'll want to hear my news."

"Go ahead, what's happened?"

"Halsey left the Commons at just gone eight o'clock last night and I followed him. He got on a District line tube train and I followed him all the way out to the end of the line at Upminster. He then walked to the Grove Lodge Hotel, a grotty little no-star place."

"And then what?"

"I hung around outside the entrance, where I could see that he was checking in. Once he had disappeared up the stairs I went inside. I had to be a bit inventive and I took a bit of a flyer."

"What do you mean? What did you do?"

"I said that I'd had a problem parking and that I'd had to box in the chap who had just come in. I said I just wanted to let him know and find out when he'd be leaving. He said that would be Mr. Jacobs and he could give him a ring. I said 'no, don't bother, I can see him and explain'."

"And so he gave you the room number?"

"Yes, room 12 on the first floor."

"You didn't pay him a visit?"

"No, of course not. I went up the stairs, nosed around a bit and then came down again."

"So then what did you do?"

"Talked to the guy at reception some more, made some small talk and then said I was interested in staying for a couple of weeks next month if he had a vacancy. He checked out dates and I waffled to him about wanting the best rate he could possibly do. Then I said I needed to check this out with my wife and I'd call her on my mobile."

"This all sounds good – you've obviously done things like this before."

"Yes, more than a few times. Anyway I take a seat and the guy goes off in to his little office behind the reception desk. I sit there, mobile to my ear, pretending to be talking to my non-existent wife."

"I like the sound of this, Jeff. I think I can almost guess where this is leading."

"Yes you probably can. I sit there for about ten minutes and then this stunning-looking lady walks in – tall, dark hair, classy dresser, legs that went on forever. Matey comes out of his office with his eyes out on stalks and asks if he can help. She says yes – her husband should have booked in, name of Mr. Jacobs."

"Matey leers at her and says 'yes, he's in room 12'. Then he stands there transfixed by her legs as she disappears up the stairs."

Simon punched the air. "Yes, I knew it! Good man."

"Well, we can't get too excited. They checked out about an hour and a half ago and got two cabs. He returned to the Commons in one and she headed off somewhere in the opposite direction in the other. Now I'm back at the Commons, sitting in my favourite corridor."

"So we now know that he spent the night in a seedy hotel room with another woman?"

"Well, yes, we do know that, but I don't have any photographic proof of just what they got up to. I'm afraid it would just be our word against his. They could have spent the whole night working on his parliamentary papers, but it's hardly likely, is it?"

"We'll get the proof, Jeff. Now we know he's got a bit on the side we know this is all worthwhile. I want you to keep following him and start thinking about how you can get some real proof the next time he sees her."

"Okay, will do. Oh, and one more thing."

"Yes?"

"While they were getting up to whatever it was they were getting up to last night, I put a call through to his home. His wife answered and I said I was calling from the Commons and that I was doing some research for her husband and needed to contact him urgently."

"And what did she say?"

"That he had a late business meeting in London and then he would be checking into a hotel. She didn't know which one, but he would be calling her later. She offered to give him a message but I said not to bother, I would keep trying his mobile."

"Very sneaky; how did you get his home number?"

"I'm a private investigator, Mr. Lake, it's what I do."

"Good stuff, well done. We're onto something now. I bet all of this is the key to why Kelly was in his car."

"We don't know how long it will be before he sees his lady friend again, though. I could be wasting a lot more of your money sitting around here."

"Don't worry about that, just keep following him everywhere he goes."

For the first time in ages Simon had a smile on his face and some hope in his heart as he stared out of the study window. He was anxious to progress things now, but he realised that he would still have to bide his time until Jeff came up with some hard evidence.

The main thing was that his hunch that Halsey was doing something he shouldn't had finally proved to be correct. Maybe he was a serial womaniser who had relationships with lots of women, and Kelly had simply been one of many. Maybe his only extramarital affair was with the woman in the hotel. The key factor was that he was playing away from home – so he had something to cover up.

CHAPTER 16

The good news was followed by bad news the following morning when Peter called from the office.

"Bad news, Simon – Charles Dalton is taking his business elsewhere."

"What? Bloody hell – he's moving his account?"

"Yes, I'm afraid so and I have to tell you I'm not best pleased. He was our biggest client and this will make a big hole in our numbers. It is very bad news for the firm."

"But why the hell has he done this? I know I've been dragging my heels a bit because of everything that's happened, but there's no great rush. It's only his year-end and we've got plenty of time."

"Yes, but there's the tax aspect as well. He's asked for advice on what to put where and you haven't provided it yet."

"Okay, I know, but it's no big deal. Bloody hell, Peter I've done a great job for Dalton over the years; saved him a fortune. I've worked every tax dodge in the book for him – and some more. I really thought that we had a long-standing relationship that would count for something in times of trouble."

"It's not just the financial aspect, Charles says he can't have his reputation sullied by links to you."

"Rubbish, absolutely bloody rubbish. I can't believe he said that. For years he's had a reputation as a rotten landlord who is only interested in screwing every last penny out of his tenants. For him to start playing mister high and mighty now is a bit bloody rich."

"Well, that's his take on things and we can't stop him taking his business away."

"I don't believe this. Let me talk to him and I'll spend the rest of the week stuck in to his work and nothing else. I'm sure I can talk him round."

"No, he's absolutely adamant. I've already spent ages trying to talk him round but he won't have it. He says you've blotted your copybook and he can't trust you to give him the same level of service he's had in the past. He's hell bent on this and I'm not going to spend any more time on my knees begging him to reconsider."

"I'm sorry – I really thought he'd be a bit more understanding. I'll come in to the office later – I'd better make sure we don't lose anyone else."

"Yes, that would be a very good idea. It's time for you to get your act together."

Click – the line went dead.

Simon was shell-shocked for a while. The Dalton account had been the cornerstone of building up the firm. He'd been a demanding client but he'd been prepared to pay for all that he had demanded. This would make a big hole in the revenue and an even bigger hole in the profits.

He knew that he did indeed have to get his act together soon and get himself back into the office. The problem was that this had made it even harder than ever. It was bad enough as it was, with all the staff giving him sideways looks and wondering if he could possibly have committed murder. Now to add to all that, the staff would all know that one of the partners had disgraced himself and lost the firm a big chunk of its most profitable business.

When the post arrived Jeff Clarke's next invoice didn't improve Simon's mood. Much of it was for travel, hotels and meals but he had to accept that at least it was all backed up by reasonable-looking receipts.

He sat at his PC and looked at the balance of his accounts in the online banking system. He had already raided his current and E-savings accounts and resigned himself to having to move some money from a term account. He would just have to lose some interest; as an accountant that really rankled, but it was a case of needs must. In the meantime he decided he would have to temporarily borrow some money from his and Pippa's joint account so that he could settle this latest bill.

When he arrived at work early that afternoon Peter immediately appeared and asked him to come in to his office for a chat. Chris was already there and it was apparent that this was to be an impromptu partners meeting. They both sat unsmiling on one side of the meeting table and Simon took the chair opposite them. He forced a smile. "This looks like a serious chat."

Peter peered over the glasses on the end of his nose. "Yes, I'm afraid it is. Chris and I have both agreed that we can't allow the current situation to drift on."

"What exactly does that mean?"

"It means that Chris and I believe we have both been very supportive of you and very tolerant through the tough time you've had."

Simon interjected. "Yes, you have and I really do appreciate that."

Peter continued. "You have to face the fact that the police may never catch the person who killed Kelly Taylor. It may just end up on their long list of unsolved crimes. Given that possibility you can't go on living like a hermit forever, Simon. You're going to have to get back to normal. It is what we think you need and it's what the firm needs."

Chris chipped in. "To be blunt, we've been carrying you while all this has been going on and we can't keep doing it. The firm has now lost its best client because of all this and we're all going to take a hefty hit in the pocket as a result."

Simon bridled. "Okay, I accept that but I think I can say that this is the first time I've ever caused the firm a problem. Set against that are all the years when I've worked bloody night and day, seven days a week. Now suddenly I have a nightmare situation to deal with, which is completely out of my control, and I think I deserve some understanding from you guys and a little bit of leeway."

Peter leaned forward. "Frankly, we think we've already given you that understanding and leeway, Simon, but now enough is enough. You are a free man – you were arrested but never charged, and that must be because the police don't think you did it."

"No, they think I did it all right, but they can't prove it. They've no evidence against me but sure as hell they're looking for it. What if they can't find anything and decide to plant some? It's happened before – there are lots of cases where an innocent man has been stitched up to save the blushes of the police."

Peter looked dismissive. "That's rubbish; you're getting paranoid. You think everyone's out to get you but if you could just go back to working normally I think you'd find life would slowly return to how it used to be."

Chris was nodding vigorously. "That's right – the longer you hide at home the tougher it will be for you to pull yourself through this."

Simon shook his head. "Try telling that to the bastard who painted graffiti on my front door and to the toe-rag who vandalised my car. Not to mention all the people who have written, emailed and phoned to let me know what a murdering bastard they think I am."

Peter smiled sympathetically. "I know it must be hard, I realise that and we have all really felt for you."

Simon slid his chair back. "So cut me some slack, you two. I'm working on something that I think will soon nail the real killer, and then I will be able to get back to something like normal."

With that he stood up and walked out, leaving Peter and Chris staring at each other and shaking their heads.

Simon spent the rest of the afternoon shut in his office. He half-heartedly looked at some emails, leafed through some of the mountain of paperwork that had piled up in his in-tray and stared idly out of the window. Jo knocked at the door and came in with a pile of paperwork.

"Can we go through some of this, please Simon? It's been piling up for a while and it's stuff that really does need to be actioned."

He glanced at it and shook his head. "Take it to Peter or Chris – they are bravely shouldering all the responsibility in this firm while their lame duck partner slopes off and buries his head in the sand."

She touched his arm. "We all hate seeing you like this – you just aren't yourself right now."

Simon scooped up the papers on his desk and stuffed them in his briefcase. "I'm sorry Jo – I'll be at home if anyone needs me."

He walked out leaving her standing there with her arms full of papers and her eyes full of tears.

He got home before Pippa; she'd said something about going shopping. When she walked in with her arms full of carrier bags her face was as black as thunder.

"What's wrong with you?"

"I've just been made to look absolutely bloody stupid in Next."

"Why, what happened?"

"I tried to pay for an outfit I'd found for Emma's christening, but it seems there's not enough in our account. I stood there insisting there must be some mistake because we always keep plenty of spending money in there. The queue was building up behind me and it was bloody embarrassing to say the least. I actually saw that cow Mary Jenkins behind me with a big smirk on her face. Now all the neighbours will know within a couple of days."

"Oh, I'm sorry, that's probably my fault. I had to temporarily move some money into my personal account while I'm waiting to get a transfer from my term account."

"What?"

"I had to move some money around and I made a mistake. I'm sorry."

"What do you mean, you had to move money around? You've always been so careful with money and we've never been caught short. You're an accountant, for Christ's sake – how can you bugger up your own bank balance?"

"Oh it's all this hassle that's going on. I took my eye off the ball. I really am sorry and I'll pay for your outfit."

Pippa was shaking her head. "I don't like the sound of all this, Simon. I want you to get in to the online banking system right now while I'm here and I want you to show me the statements for the last month for all our accounts."

"Bloody hell, so you're an auditor all of a sudden, are you?"

"No, I'm a worried wife whose husband has been doing some bloody daft things lately. I want to know what is going on, Simon, and I want to know just where our money has been going."

"Can't you just trust me?"

"No, I'm not sure I can any more. I used to – never had a doubt about you, but right now you are acting so weird it scares the hell out of me."

"Look, it's just that I've had to make some enquiries."

"What does that mean? What enquiries?"

"I needed to find out more about Halsey."

Her eyes narrowed. "I don't like the sound of this. What do you mean, exactly?"

He looked down. "Well, the police didn't seem to be getting anywhere. They didn't even seem to be trying once Halsey came up with his alibi."

"And?"

"And so I decided to find out if Halsey has a secret life – something he might need to cover up. Just because he didn't actually murder her himself doesn't mean that he wasn't responsible for her death in some way."

"And so what have you done?"

"I hired a surveillance man to find out."

Pippa looked ready to explode. "You bloody idiot. Is there no end to this? So are you telling me that is why I couldn't pay for a sodding dress in Next? Because you've been spending our money on a bloody private eye?"

"I just needed to borrow a bit from our joint account – because of a temporary cash flow problem. By tomorrow I'll have transferred some money from my term account and then you can buy all the dresses you want."

"In all the years I've been married to you the one thing I've never felt I had to worry about was money, Simon. I know we struggled at first to save some money and get on to the property ladder. There wasn't much coming in during the early days of the firm but I always felt that you knew for sure that we could cover all of our bills. I used to think how funny it is that everyone laughs about the stereotypical accountant's image, but I just loved it.

I always figured you knew so much about money and how to balance books that we'd never ever have any financial problems. Now I find out you're blowing our hard-earned savings on something you should never have got involved in. Whatever next, for God's sake? Are you going to start your own police force?"

"I just need to clear my name, and actually the guy I hired has already come up with the goods."

"What does that mean?"

"He followed Halsey to a seedy little hotel in Upminster, where he spent the night with a stunning-looking woman who wasn't his wife."

"And so? Don't half the politicians in Westminster get up to things like that? And anyway, how the hell are you going to link his bit of nooky with the murder of Kelly Taylor?"

"Well, don't you see? He's got a bit on the side – Kelly Taylor was seen in his car. Maybe he was having an affair with her too – or maybe she was blackmailing him. Maybe she knew all about this other woman and was threatening to tell the lovely Louisa."

"So many maybes. Maybe you can screw up his marriage with this little bit of scandal, but I don't see how you can pin a murder on him."

"Well, I think there's a lot still to find out. We're going to get some photographic evidence of exactly what he's up to and then I'm taking it to Whitley. I'll push him into taking some action and getting to the bottom of just what's been going on."

"So you're going to continue spending money on this private eye of yours?"

"Yes, but not much. I think I'm nearly there."

"Well, I think you're nearly ready for the bloody loony bin. You need to tell Whitley what you've found out and you need to get back to work and stop bloody wasting our money."

"All in good time, darling. Just bear with me for a few more days please, that's all I ask."

Pippa had heard enough. She stomped up the stairs and slammed the bedroom door so hard the wall shook for several seconds.

Simon sat in the study, staring at the computer screen. He was looking at an Excel spreadsheet that showed a summary of all of his financial assets. It was all very straightforward stuff to a chartered accountant. He could see at a glance all of his assets and his liabilities, the totals they added up to and the net difference.

He had always loved numbers. He lived and died by them. Simon took great comfort from looking at how the firm was performing and the spin-off from this into his own personal world. His spreadsheets were like a sort of financial electro-cardiogram.

When the assets comfortably exceeded the liabilities then life was comfortable, safe and secure. However, should the opposite happen then he knew that alarm bells would ring and doctors and nurses would run around inside his head. For many years now he had only ever seen good news on the screen in front of him.

CHAPTER 17

When Simon came downstairs the next morning there was a note on the kitchen table.

'I've gone to stay with Chloe for a few days. There's plenty of food in the fridge. I'll be back when I know my old Simon has returned. Love P.'

He made some coffee and then read the note again, several times. Eventually he screwed it up, threw it in the bin and headed for the study.

Jeff Clarke called with his latest update.

"Hi Jeff, what's news?"

"Nothing, I'm afraid. He's back to the old routine of meetings, meetings and more bloody meetings."

"No sign of the mystery woman?"

"None at all; he seems far too busy to be doing anything naughty. Maybe he only sees her once a month?"

"Don't say that, Jeff. I can't afford to pay for another month of you clocking up huge bills."

"Well, there's no way of knowing, is there, Mr. Lake? He might see her tonight and then again he might never see her again."

"I can't believe that, can you? She didn't sound like a one-night stand."

"No, and she certainly didn't look like a one-night stand. My gut feeling is that this has all been going on for quite a while."

"So when he does see her next, how are you going to get me some evidence?"

"Oh, I'm keeping a camera with me all the time now, and it's very clever, very unobtrusive."

"Okay Jeff – keep at it and call me as soon as you have anything."

That afternoon he received a surprise call.

"Hello, Mr. Lake. It's Jayne here: you might remember me, I own 'Flowers For You'. I've come across something you might be interested in."

He sat bolt upright. "Hello Jayne. What is it?"

"I'd rather not say over the phone. Would you like to come to the shop, after we close tonight?"

"Yes, sure, what time?"

"Well, we close at 5.30 and all the girls are gone by six. I stay on to cash up and catch up on paperwork so if you like, knock on the door at around seven."

"Okay Jayne, I'll be there."

"Oh and Mr. Lake – this will have to be just between us. I don't want anyone else to know. I'm simply going to show you a piece of paper, nothing more."

Simon spent the next few hours wondering what would be on the piece of paper. He wondered if this might be the breakthrough he needed. He wondered why Jayne was talking to him and not to DI Whitley. Maybe somebody had finally taken pity on him and figured he deserved a bit of help.

At seven o'clock on the dot he was knocking on the shop door. Jayne unlocked it, peered up and down the deserted street and ushered him through to the back office. There was paperwork all over the place – ledgers, orders, bills and correspondence. She pulled out a chair for him and they sat one either side of a big wooden farmhouse-style table.

She looked at him as if second-guessing whether she was doing the right thing.

"Mr. Lake, I'm going to show you a piece of paper but you can't take it away with you. I won't even let you copy it and I will deny ever showing it to you if anyone should ever ask me about it. Is that understood?"

Simon nodded eagerly. "I understand – and by the way, it's Simon, not Mr. Lake."

She smiled warily. "Okay then, Simon it is. But I want you to understand something first. What my customers do is entirely up to them. They send flowers for many different reasons and it's not my job to ever question whether they should be doing whatever it is they are doing. Often they give us false details – they don't give their right name or address. "

Simon nodded. "I can understand that."

Jayne looked at him. "Sometimes it's a real pain when there is a problem delivering something. We might try calling the sender to check the address but then we find they've given us a false phone number. They rarely pay by card or cheque – cash is anonymous."

"Does this happen a lot when people send flowers to somebody they aren't married to?"

"Yes, particularly if that person is married to someone else."

"So what would happen if someone came in here demanding to see the order form for their flowers?"

"We wouldn't show it to them. It is private between the sender and us."

"Aren't there any exceptions?"

"Only the situation I told you about before - when the police are involved. We get an occasional stalking situation where a woman might get lots of flowers from some nutter and she gets really scared. We had one fifty-year-old man who kept sending red roses to a thirteen- year-old schoolgirl. If the police demand information then I will always give it to them, but only after I've seen a warrant card."

"Okay, I promise I'll respect your confidentiality and I'm really grateful that you've decided to show me whatever it is."

She nodded and pulled an order form from a thick file. "This was an order placed by a customer of interest to you some months ago. The order was placed here in the shop and we relayed it to a florist in London, near the delivery address."

Simon read it through carefully. The recipient's name was Lucy Tomlinson and the delivery address was DeLaCruz Vernaille Marketing, 12 Stag Place West, London SW1. The message to go with the flowers was 'Next time don't get so close to the radiator. I love you so much. M xxx'

Simon looked up. "What does 24 RR HT mean?"

"Oh, that is the actual requirement as written by the florist who took the order. It means a 24 red rose hand-tied bouquet. It was an expensive order."

"So I see – a penny short of a hundred quid."

"Yes, £95 for the flowers plus a £4.99 relay charge."

"What does 'PC' mean?"

"Paid cash."

Simon studied the form some more. "Why did he write the message on the form? I usually write on the card myself when I buy flowers for my wife and then I put the card in the envelope and seal it."

"Because it was a relay order. We enter the message on the computer, send it and then it gets printed out at the receiving florist's end."

He nodded. "There is a contact telephone number here for the sender. I wonder what would happen if we tried it?"

Jayne smiled. "I already have."

"And what happened?"

"Number unobtainable."

Simon continued looking at the form. "What do you think the card message means?"

Jayne smiled again and reddened slightly. "I don't know. One can only guess. I suppose that in a passionate situation, with not many clothes on, you could get burnt."

Simon grinned, embarrassed by his own naivety. "The sender's name, Hary Semlak, looks odd. There are two rs in Harry, why not make up something better?"

"Do you like crosswords?"

"Yes."

"So do I. I love anagrams."

Simon peered at the name some more until the penny finally dropped. "You're obviously a lot better at them than me. Just one more question, Jayne. Whose handwriting is this on the form?"

"Kelly's."

"Thanks, I really appreciate this. Why didn't you give it to the police?"

"Because I read the bit in the paper, about how you felt they weren't working hard enough to clear your name. I figured maybe you deserved a little bit of help."

He wanted to kiss her but decided against it. "Thank you so much. I can't tell you how much I appreciate this."

She opened the door and smiled. "I haven't done anything and I don't want us to ever meet or talk again."

"I won't let you down. I give you my word."

As soon as Simon got back to his car he pulled a notepad and pen out of the glove compartment. He wrote down the name and address of Lucy Tomlinson, which he had very carefully memorised.

Jeff would be impressed that he had found out the woman's name and address, although he wondered if he really needed Jeff's services any more. He figured he could progress things himself and save an awful lot of money in the process.

He decided to sleep on it and then first thing the next morning he called Jeff on his mobile. He told him he now had enough evidence and asked Jeff to send him his final invoice. He was disappointed and quizzed Simon as to why he didn't wait a little longer to get the photographic evidence he wanted. A nice little earner for him had come to a premature end.

Simon actually knew where Stag Place West was. At one time he had a client whose office was in Victoria Street, and when Simon visited him he would use the underground car park around the corner from the office in Stag Place. He thought he could almost envisage the building Lucy Tomlinson worked in.

Jeff had told him as much as he knew about what was in Halsey's diary for the next few days. He was in the Commons all day today and then attending a cancer charity function at a hotel in Oxford. He was staying there overnight and then returning home for a constituency surgery tomorrow.

Simon gazed out of the window, wondering what to do next. Somehow he had to catch Halsey with his mistress and get some evidence of their affair. There was no telling when he would see her next and so there was nothing for it but to follow him and bide his time. He moved through to the bedroom and started packing an overnight bag.

He called the hotel in Oxford and booked himself a single room for one night. The drive took most of the afternoon and he checked in just after four o'clock. The Bluebell Lodge was actually a typical modern three-star hotel, although the grounds looked more impressive than the norm for a business hotel. There was a function board in reception listing the day's events. There were four different events listed, including 'United Cancer Action' – The De Vere Room.

Simon glanced at the board as he registered at the desk. He smiled at the girl behind the desk. "That's a good cause – I often donate money to them."
She smiled back at him. "Yes – they have an annual dinner here. All the board members and patrons get together."
        "Is it mainly business or pleasure?"

"A bit of both I think. They talk shop for a while and then have a dinner, with speeches, followed by a fund-raising auction."

"What time does it all start?"

"They've got a drinks reception at 7.30."

"Is it just the charity bigwigs or do they bring partners as well?"

"Most of them bring partners. All our doubles and twins are fully booked tonight."

He settled in to his room, had a shower and then changed into a casual shirt and chinos before heading back down to the reception area. He took a seat in an armchair in the corner that gave him a good view of the front entrance and the reception desk. He knew he might be in for a long wait but he had a book with him and he made a start on the Telegraph crossword.

It was just gone six when Mark and Louisa Halsey swept in. He was in a grey pin-stripe suit and Simon felt a pang of envy as he looked at just how perfectly it fitted. His blonde hair was perfectly groomed and his skin glistened as if he had just applied moisturiser. Louisa looked stunning in a tan-coloured trouser suit and high heels. Her long black hair shone under the lights and the obligatory sunglasses perched on top of her head completed the look. Simon wondered why on earth Halsey felt the need for a mistress.

They were instantly recognised by the manager and welcomed as if they were minor royalty. A porter brought in three cases and several suits and dresses on hangers. Simon wondered how much luggage they would take for two weeks holiday.

Other people appeared and greeted them like long-lost friends. Simon hid behind the Telegraph and listened as keenly as he could. He had to admire Halsey's style as he smiled, shook hands and kissed cheeks like the expert networker he obviously was. Halsey asked the receptionist for the Times and the Telegraph to be delivered in the morning and requested an early alarm call for 6 o'clock. The receptionist told him they were in a suite, room number 24, and that fresh flowers and fruit had been put in the room with the compliments of the hotel.

Simon wondered what else he could usefully get out of hanging around overnight. With Louisa present he clearly wouldn't be catching Halsey playing away from home. He knew they were headed back home in the morning, ready for his surgery with constituents. He wondered briefly whether it was worth the overnight stay but decided he would just watch and learn what he could about the Halsey lifestyle.

He wandered outside to check the car park and sure enough there was Halsey's silver S class Mercedes, the car he'd been seen in with Kelly. He looked briefly in the passenger's window, wondering yet again about quite what she'd been doing there that day. Having seen Halsey in the flesh Simon could understand why women were attracted to him. Even given the age gap he could easily have impressed a girl like Kelly.

Back in the hotel he had a sandwich and a drink in the bar and then found himself a chair that afforded a good view of the De Vere room. When the Halsey's appeared they looked like some glitzy couple at a film premiere. Louisa looked stunning in a long black sequinned ball-gown. Her husband was dressed in a dinner jacket over a whiter-than-white dress shirt.

Simon watched as they expertly schmoozed their way around the other guests. He had to admire the way that Halsey drew admiring glances from everyone as he engaged in mini conversations with each person in turn before moving on. Simon wondered if he had ever studied the Bill Clinton technique for working a room.

The doors to the De Vere room were closed once the formal meeting and dinner got under way. Simon had another drink in the bar and then booked an alarm call for 6 o'clock and headed for his room. He watched TV for a while and wondered if he should call Pippa. Deciding that he didn't want to have to explain where he was and why, he went to bed.

CHAPTER 18

There was no sign of the Halseys at breakfast but Simon watched them check out at just gone seven. He wondered briefly if he should attempt to follow them in his car but figured out that it would be pointless. He knew where they were going anyway, so he set off ahead of them. Even driving at nearly ninety on the M40, Simon didn't have to wait long until the silver Mercedes swept past. Louisa was driving and Halsey was on the phone.

Halsey held his constituency surgery in the local village hall at Hanley, but there was no sign of his car when Simon arrived. He parked at the far end of the car park and hid behind his newspaper. It wasn't long before Halsey appeared and Simon figured he must have gone via home as he was on his own. There were only two other cars to be seen but through the morning various people came and went. Simon wondered how seriously Halsey took his constituents' problems – did he follow them up assiduously or was it a rubber stamp job, just being seen to do the right thing?

For one mad moment, when it seemed that the last constituent had left, Simon actually wondered whether he should go in. He could pretend that he was the next person with a problem wanting to see Mr. Fixit. Then when he was alone with him he could challenge him over Kelly and let him know that he knew all about Lucy Tomlinson. No – it was too soon. Halsey would only bluff it out and it would put him on his guard. Simon knew that he needed real photographic proof before he would get anything out of him.

When Halsey left the hall Simon let him get well down the road before he followed, but he had difficulty catching up. Halsey was doing a good fifty miles an hour through the village. The thirty limit signs meant nothing to him and he didn't even slow down as he passed the primary school. As Simon neared Hanley Mansion the electronic gates were already closing, and he just caught a brief glimpse of the Mercedes sweeping up the drive to the majestic Tudor mansion.

Simon pulled off the road at the first opportunity, into an entrance to a field. It took him some time to walk all around the estate that was Hanley Mansion. He was very wary of cameras – Halsey was sure to have a state-of-the-art security system. There was a high stone wall that ran all the way around. There were two heavy wooden doors set in to the wall at different points to the rear of the grounds – he felt certain they would both be locked and bolted, but he didn't dare try them. He could see that each door was covered by a camera, mounted high up on top of the wall.

Although he returned home that night, Simon spent the next few days tracking Halsey from Hanley to Westminster to Ipswich to Hanley and then back to Westminster again. Jeff had been right – the man was a human dynamo. Forever in meetings or on the move, he made more phone calls in a day than Simon ever did in a week. Simon kept his digital camera with him at all times but had no cause to use it.

It was the following Tuesday before there was a break in the routine. Simon had followed Halsey to Bury St. Edmunds, where he had attended a business meeting in a hotel near the cathedral on Angel Hill. Halsey's car was in the hotel car park, but as he left the building early that afternoon he shook hands with various men in suits and then walked around the corner towards the town centre. He looked at his watch, went to the bank and then walked around WH Smith for a while, browsing through magazines. He looked at his watch again and then headed back to the hotel.

Halsey walked back to the hotel car park but went straight past his Mercedes and opened the passenger door of a blue Audi saloon. Simon gasped as he saw Halsey lean across and kiss a woman in the driver's seat. She looked young, with dark hair, and she immediately started the engine. It was hard to tell but the woman appeared to match Jeff's description of the woman in Upminster. His heart racing, Simon got back to his car and followed the Audi out of Bury and on to the A134.

Simon kept well back, but from the angle of their heads he thought they were busy talking and hopefully she wouldn't be spending much time looking in the rear-view mirror. They were headed in the Thetford direction and when they reached Thetford Forest the Audi took a right turn at a 'Picnic Site' sign. Simon slowed right down and let the Audi disappear down the track ahead.

He left it a minute and then crawled slowly down the track. There were little clearings off to the side, large enough for just one or two cars to pull in for a picnic. Some were quite open but some were well covered with trees and foliage. It was the perfect place – they had surely been there before. He saw just the tail end of a blue car, its brake lights went off. It was down one of the more secluded turn-offs. Simon drove slowly to the next turning and parked.

He felt his heart thumping as he took the camera from the glove compartment and made his way back through the trees. If anyone saw him they would surely think he was a pervert, out to catch a couple in a car. That was exactly what he was doing but Simon didn't feel like a perv – he just felt very very scared about what he was attempting to do.

He approached the car slowly and carefully from the rear on the driver's side. There was no sign of anyone else and Simon winced at the noise of a twig breaking as he stepped on it. They had picked their spot well - it was very secluded. There was plenty of cover for Simon to hide behind, but he felt that every time he put a foot down he was sure to be heard. As he edged closer he saw that all the car windows were fully up and he just hoped that they had some noise coming from a radio or a CD in there.

He reached the last tree before the car and, peering through the branches, he could see they were in the front seats, embracing. Simon tried to keep calm as he readied his camera, worried about the noise it would make. He knew it emitted a low beeping noise as the shutter button was depressed but it was much quieter than his previous camera.

He edged slightly closer and was now just some twenty feet away. He could see the back of the woman's head but not Halsey's face – they were kissing passionately. Simon took his first picture. The sound was much louder than he remembered but thankfully there was also the faint sound of music coming from the car. The heads didn't move and the two seemed intent only on each other. Simon took his second picture.

The driver's door opened and the music was louder. The woman got out, her short skirt riding high above her long legs. Her hair was tousled and the top buttons of her white blouse were undone. Simon held his breath as he took the third picture. The camera sounded louder than the music but she didn't notice. Halsey stepped out of the passenger door and Simon got a shot of his head above the roof of the car. The two of them opened the rear doors and climbed in.

The woman had only half-closed the door behind her and they started kissing again. Simon could see the skirt riding ever higher up her legs and when he took the next picture Halsey's hand was visible on her thigh.

The woman pulled the door shut behind her and the two of them were animatedly moving around inside. Simon realised they were getting ready to go all the way and he felt scared and embarrassed by his own voyeurism.

There was lots of movement as the two groped each other and they seemed to be helping each other to get partially undressed. The woman straddled Halsey and started to move up and down as Simon took several more pictures. After a few minutes the action subsided and both rear doors opened. They both climbed out on the side nearest Simon – looking hot and giggling loudly, like a pair of teenagers. Halsey had his shirt hanging out and he was trying unsuccessfully to pull up his trousers. Simon clicked away some more. The woman pulled her pants on and tugged her skirt down to a respectable level.

He moved to take one last shot and it was then that he stepped on the branch. The snapping sound was like a rifle shot and he froze. The lovers both looked towards him. Halsey shouted "What the hell!" and the woman screamed. Simon was already moving – the game was up. He ran towards his car and as he looked back he saw Halsey hopping on one leg as he struggled to get his trousers on. The woman was screaming hysterically.

Simon reached his car, wrenched open the door, dived in and started the engine. He reversed back along the narrow track and then spun the wheels as he headed back toward the main road. Halsey ran out of the side turning just as Simon was passing it – his shirt still hanging out and with no shoes on - with a lump of wood in his hand. He hit the windscreen a glancing blow as Simon tore past and shouted out "You bastard, you bloody pervert!"

He drove home as fast as he could, heart thumping and eyes constantly checking the rear-view mirror. He figured he had a good start on Halsey as he would have had to return to his car and finish dressing. As soon as he got to the house he put the car in the garage and ran indoors with his precious camera. He could only hope that Halsey hadn't taken the registration number – in the panic and confusion it seemed unlikely.

It was a long time before Simon's heartbeat returned to something like normal. He had a stiff drink and headed for the study. Switching the computer on, he connected a USB cable to the camera and started downloading the pictures. He had taken seventeen in all and, although some of them weren't very clear, there were eleven good ones that showed conclusively what the pair had been up to. There were good shots of both their faces in several of them – certainly good enough to convince anyone of their identities. He knew that he had the evidence he'd been after.

Simon stared at the pictures and wondered quite what to do next. He could take them to DI Whitley as evidence that Mark Halsey was having an affair. He was sure that the woman was Lucy Tomlinson – the same woman Halsey had sent flowers to and the same woman he had spent a night with at a grubby little hotel in Upminster. The other person who had known about Lucy Tomlinson was Kelly Taylor – and she was dead.

If he went to Whitley he knew that he would be disapproving of Simon playing amateur detective. Whitley would be miffed that he had found out something that he didn't know. Also he had given Jayne his word that he wouldn't divulge what she had shown him on the order form for Lucy's flowers. If he couldn't tell Whitley about that link between Kelly and Halsey then he didn't have much chance of convincing him anyway. Whitley would say that all he had found out was that an MP, who allegedly had once been seen with Kelly, was having an affair. He would point out that many MPs had elicit affairs, that Halsey had a cast-iron alibi for the morning Kelly was killed, and that any link via a third party only existed inside Simon's head.

No, the only way to proceed was to tackle Halsey direct. He would present him with the photographic evidence and then he would explain that he knew Kelly had taken his order for flowers to go to Lucy Tomlinson. Then he would challenge him to deny that he wasn't linked to Kelly Taylor's death in some way.

He picked up the phone and rang Halsey's secretary. "Hello, my name is John Stevens. I'm a constituent of Mr. Halsey's and I have a problem I think he could help me with. Could I arrange to see him when he has his next surgery please?"

"Could I take some details first sir?"

Simon had anticipated that she would check the electoral roll or something to ascertain that he really was a constituent. Consequently he had taken a chance and used a neighbour's name and address. After a delay, when Simon guessed she was checking on her computer, she finally seemed satisfied.

"What is the nature of your problem, Mr. Stevens?"

"I want to make a donation to the Conservative Party but first I want to check that the nature of the donation I have in mind is ethical and above board. I've read all about cash for honours scandals and I don't wish to be associated with that sort of thing in any way."

Simon was sure Halsey would want to talk to anyone who was planning to give his party some money.

"Yes, I'm sure Mr. Halsey will be delighted to see you. He is having another surgery at Hanley village hall in about two weeks' time, on Tuesday, 17th March. I could slot you in for 10 o'clock – how would that be?"

"That is excellent. Will you be sending me some sort of confirmation?"

"Oh yes, Mr. Stevens, I always do."

"Good – instead of sending it my home address could you please address it care of The Gables in Chiltern Avenue, Ipswich. I'm staying with some friends temporarily while the builders install new central heating in my house."

"Yes of course, Mr. Stevens, no problem at all."

CHAPTER 19

Armed with Jeff Clarke's final invoice and the photos, Simon visited him to settle up and check one last thing. Clarke was pleased with the cheque Simon handed him – he obviously wasn't used to clients paying quite so promptly.

"So, Mr. Lake, is there anything else I can do for you?"

"Just one more thing."

Simon pulled the pictures out of an envelope and spread them on the table. "Tell me, is that the woman Halsey slept with in Upminster?"

Jeff whistled. "Wow, it certainly is. Isn't she a cracker? You've done well – where did you get these?"

Simon smiled. "I was bird-watching in Thetford Forest."

"Indeed you were, Mr. Lake, indeed you were. You should pack in the accountancy lark and come and work here."

Simon grinned. "I don't think so. I didn't much enjoy being a peeping Tom – I think I'm getting too old for this sort of caper, but it paid off."

Jeff stood and shook his hand. "Goodbye, Mr. Lake – I really do wish you well. Let me know if there is ever anything else I can do for you."

When he got back home the phone was ringing.

"Hello Simon, it's Peter. I don't suppose there's any chance of you coming in and doing some work, is there?"

"Oh, hello Peter. Look, I'm really sorry – I had to go away for a few days but I've achieved what I needed to."

"What does that mean exactly?"

"I've had to do a bit of investigation work and now I've found what I was looking for."

"Do you want to tell me about it?"

"No, I'm sorry – I can't tell anyone about it just yet. All I can say is that I've uncovered the secret life of one of the suspects in Kelly's murder. A secret life that gives him a motive to kill."

"And what is the view of the police about all this, Simon?"

"Oh, even they don't know yet. I'm having to work on it myself to stop them fouling things up."

"Look, old man, don't you think that all this amateur sleuthing is getting a bit ridiculous?"

"No, I've got to look out for myself. I'm still getting hate mail – there are still lots of people out there convinced I did it and until I prove them wrong I can't get on with life. I'm sorry, but that's the way it is."

"Simon, I hate to have to say this, but there are three partners in this firm. Two of us are working our butts off, night and day, to cover for the third partner, who seems to have gone walkabout. Quite frankly, Chris and I have just about had enough – we're at our wits' end. We need you back here pulling your weight."

"Well, you're just going to have to wait a bit longer until I sort things out."

"Then if you're not prepared to totally commit yourself to the firm any more maybe we should talk about your departure."

"Oh no – soon I'll have cleared my name and then I'll be back. Until then you're just going to have to soldier on without me."

"We can't wait indefinitely."

"I'm sorry, but you'll have to give me another couple of weeks. I've got to go – I'll be in touch."

"Before you go, one more thing. Charles Dalton wants all his paperwork back – he wants to get his new accountant to crack on but he says he can't until he gets all his files and stuff back that you've got at home."

"Yeah, okay, when I get a chance I'll box it all up, but it's not at the top of my list of priorities right now."

He put the phone down and went back to staring out of the study window.

He felt let down that Peter and Chris were starting to put the pressure on him. For years it had been rare for anyone to put in more hours than he had. Now that he had hit trouble, through no fault of his own, he expected the rest of the firm to give him some leeway and help him through this. He figured he was on his own.

The next call was from Paul. "Hi Dad, how are you? I've been worried about you."

"Hi Paul, not bad I guess. I'm making some progress. I've been doing some checking and now I've really got something on Mark Halsey, the MP who was seen with Kelly in his car."

"You sound like a detective, Dad."

"I'm starting to feel like one."

"I spoke to Mum last night. She's still at Chloe's – she's really worried about you."

"She thinks I'm going nuts, doesn't she?"

"She's worried that you've got things all out of proportion. She told me about the private eye."

"I'm not using him any more, I've paid him off. I'm doing my own checking now and it's paying dividends."

"Are you going to work?"

"Not right now, but I'll be back when I've got all this sorted."

"Mum wondered why you hadn't called her. She's been trying to ring you but not getting any answer."

"I've been away for a few days. I'll probably call her tonight."

"Dad, this doesn't sound like you. You've been so close to Mum all through my life – I've never known you go a day without talking to her, no matter where you were."

"Oh, we just had a bit of a domestic, it'll pass."

"She told me you were spending a bundle on this private detective and that worried her."

"Well, it needn't worry anyone. I told you – I've paid him off now. You don't need to worry about me, you'll still get your inheritance."

That really stung Paul. "Please don't talk like that – that's not what I'm worried about. I just want you to get back to being my old Dad again. That's all Mum, Chloe and me are worried about – sod the money, it's got absolutely nothing to do with money."

"I just need some space for now, Paul. I'll be in touch."

He put the phone down and went to the kitchen to fix himself a large G&T – he wished everyone would just get on with their own lives and leave him be.

Over the next few days Simon rehearsed what he planned to say to Mark Halsey over and over again. He printed off the pictures and carefully arranged them into chronological order in a clear plastic file. He wondered whether Halsey saw constituents on a one-to-one basis or whether there was always a secretary present. If there was, then he would just have to say that the matter he wished to discuss was personal and he didn't want anyone else there.

The night before he was due to see Halsey, Simon consumed his usual large G&T and then sat down to an instant microwaved spaghetti bolognaise, accompanied by a bottle of Merlot. The alcohol put him into a melancholy mood and he dialled Chloe's number.

"Hello Dad, you've been very elusive."

"Yes, sorry – I've been a bit preoccupied."

"What's happening, are you back at work?"

"Not yet, but I will be soon."

"Have you been drinking?"

"Just a few glasses of wine with a meal, is that allowed?"

"Mum's really worried about you – we all are."

"I know. It'll all be sorted soon, though. Does your Mum want to talk to me?"

"Yes, of course she does, she's right here."

"Okay, pass me over Chloe – and don't worry about me. I'll be okay, I promise."

The phone was passed to Pippa. "Hello darling, how are you?"

"I'm okay – I'm getting somewhere. Things will come to a head tomorrow."

"How, what's happening?"

"I'm going to see Mark Halsey – I'm going to show him a set of pictures of him and his mistress having sex in the back of her car."

"What? How the hell is that going to help anyone? Are you completely nuts?"

"I'm going to challenge him – he's screwing around. Kelly Taylor found out and now she's dead. I just want him to explain how and why she came to be seen in his car. I've got him over a barrel, Pippa – he's the killer and I'm going to nail him."

"That is absolutely bloody mad. You have to let the police do that – you're acting like a vigilante."

"Just let me do this my way. I've done a lot of work on this, a lot of thinking. I think I'm about to clear my name and then maybe everyone will leave me alone and let me get on with my life."

"This is totally bloody crazy. In the unlikely event that Halsey hired some hit man to kill her he could have the same person get rid of you. If Kelly was blackmailing him or something then maybe he'll stop at nothing."

"I've thought all that through. He'll know the pictures are on a digital camera and a computer and I'll tell him that for my own safety I've also lodged copies with a third party. He won't be able to destroy the evidence by having me bumped off."

"I can't believe we're even talking this way. It's like something out of a movie, for God's sake."

"Don't worry, darling. I'll call you again when I've got any more news."

"Simon, this really is total madness. I'm tempted to phone Whitley and tell him what you're planning."

"Don't you dare – I'd never forgive you. What I've told you is in the strictest confidence and I expect you to support me. I'm close to getting this whole mess sorted."

"Well, for heaven's sake be careful and promise me you'll ring and tell me what happened just as soon as you possibly can."

He poured himself a large brandy and sat in the study with all the lights turned off.

When he awoke the following morning he had a headache and felt really sluggish. He took two paracetamol with a glass of milk and a banana for breakfast. He showered and shaved and checked yet again that he had all the photos in the file in the correct order.

CHAPTER 20

He arrived at Hanley village hall ten minutes before his appointment and parked next to Halsey's Mercedes. There were only two other cars in the car park and one of those was familiar from the previous time he was there; probably it belonged to Halsey's secretary. He sat in the car, feeling the tension build, until one minute before the hour and then he got out and walked purposefully into the hall.

Halsey's secretary was what he expected – a leggy blonde in a short skirt. She smiled. "Mr. Stevens?"

"Yes, that's right."

"Mr. Halsey will see you in just a minute. He has someone with him right now but I think they're nearly finished."

She kept her mobile in one hand as if it had become permanently attached and sorted out piles of paperwork on a trestle table with the other. After a few minutes the adjoining door opened and an elderly lady was shown out by a smiling Halsey.

"I'll talk to the planning people, Mrs. Wright, and I promise you I will express your concerns in the strongest possible terms."

"Thank you – it just can't be allowed. It's an absolute disgrace."

Halsey ushered her out and glanced at Simon.

Legs flashed a smile at her boss. "This is Mr. Stevens."

Halsey beamed and held out his hand, giving the perfect handshake – dry, firm but not too strong. "Good morning, Mr. Stevens, please come in."

The room was starkly furnished with a trestle table surrounded by cheap stackable plastic chairs. Halsey motioned for Simon to take a seat and then took the chair opposite him. "So, Mr.

Stevens, I understand that you are interested in making a donation to the Conservative party?"

Simon's heart was thumping. "Actually, I want to discuss something else with you, something personal."

Halsey frowned. "I see, what would that be?"

Simon placed the plastic file on the table if front of Halsey. "I think you should look at these."

Halsey pulled out the pictures and his demeanour changed immediately. "What the hell?"

He leafed through them, his brow furrowed and his face reddening. He stared at Simon. "It was you, wasn't it – the bloody pervert?"

"I was collecting evidence."

"What the hell do you mean? Evidence of what?"

"Evidence that you are a man with something to hide."

"So what is this? A blackmail attempt?"

"No – I certainly don't want any money from you."

"So what the hell do you want?"

"I want to know what you were doing with Kelly Taylor in your car."

There was a sharp intake of breath. "She wasn't in my car. I know some girl has said she'd seen us together but she was wrong. I was questioned by the police and I was able to prove that on the morning she was killed I was in a London hotel – with my wife."

"Yes, I know all that – but there's far more to it than that, isn't there? I know that Kelly Taylor took your order for flowers to be sent to your mistress."

Halsey was staring unblinkingly at Simon. "I've just realised who you are. You're Simon Lake, the one who found her, aren't you?"

"Yes, I am – and ever since I found her body I've been hounded and vilified. I am one hundred per cent innocent and yet the police can't find the killer – because they arrested me then most people assume I must have done it."

"So what the hell are you doing – trying to succeed where the police haven't?"

"Yes, that's it exactly. You were a suspect too and as far as I'm concerned you still are."

"Rubbish, I told you I have a cast-iron alibi."

"You have an alibi for where you were, but plenty of people pay others to do their dirty work for them."

Halsey's face darkened. He shouted: "Preposterous – do you think I would have hired a hit man to kill a girl in a florist shop who just happened to know I sent flowers to a lady who isn't my wife?"

There was a tap at the door and Legs looked in. "Everything okay in here – anything you want?"

She'd heard the raised voice of her boss and probably wondered if some mad constituent was trying to assault him.

Halsey regained his composure. "No, it's okay Sally. I'll shout if I need you."

She looked at Simon, probably trying to assess whether he looked dangerous, or mad, or perhaps both. She closed the door but they both knew it was a safe bet she'd have her ear glued to it on the other side.

Simon lowered his voice. "I know Kelly was in your car. I don't know if you were having an affair with her too, or if she was working as an escort. Maybe she was just looking to make the most out of the fact that she knew you were being a bad boy and playing away from home."

For the first time Simon thought Halsey looked uneasy, rather than just angry. He followed up with his next thrust. "Did the police do a DNA check on you or your car?"

"That's between the police and me. Why the hell should I tell you?"

"Because if you won't tell me why she was in your car then I'm going to the police anyway. I'll hand over these pictures to them and then I think they will be asking you some very tough questions and carrying out some very detailed DNA tests."

This really rattled Halsey. He was quick to regain his composure but Simon knew from studying his face that this had been a telling punch.

Halsey spoke in a whisper. "We need to talk somewhere else. I can explain, but not here."

Simon was gaining in confidence – he actually had the upper hand on the urbane Mark Halsey MP. "Where do you suggest?"

"As you come off the A14, at the Norwich Road leading in to Ipswich, there's a car park on the left, where B&Q is."

"I know it."

"I'll meet you there at eight this evening."

"How do I know I'll be safe? How do I know you won't send a heavy along?"

"I'll be on my own."

"Okay, but I'll let someone else know where I am and they'll be watching to make sure you don't pull any stunts."

Halsey stood up, shaking his head as he opened the door. Legs was watching nervously as Simon walked out without another word.

He drove home and wondered if he really should confide in someone else. He wondered about calling John Black but decided against it – a lawyer wouldn't agree to act as a minder for a client playing the detective. No he would just have to chance it – Halsey wasn't to know that there wasn't someone else sitting in a car watching them both.

Simon spent the afternoon in his study mentally replaying the conversation with Halsey and trying to analyse his responses.

He wondered if he should have pushed harder for answers while Halsey was on the back foot, with Legs trying to listen at the door. Maybe he had simply given him time to concoct a plausible story. It was too late now – he would just have to play it by ear.

Late afternoon the doorbell rang. It was the garage returning his car and collecting the hire car. He briefly checked the new paint job and signed the form on the driver's clipboard. He was pleased that he would be meeting Halsey with a different car – he would probably have noted the vehicle Simon was in when he drove away from Hanley. He was starting to feel like some sort of detective – he even wondered briefly about whether he should buy some sort of recording device to collect evidence that night.

It was dark when Simon pulled into the car park just before eight. Halsey's car was already there and Simon was glad to see several other cars around and people coming and going from the different retail outlets. He parked with two other cars between him and Halsey and then walked across, opening the rear nearside door of the Mercedes and sliding in.

Halsey turned around. "What's wrong with the front seat?"

"I want to keep some distance between us. I'm not taking any chances."

Halsey actually smiled – trying to regain the upper hand. "Look, Mr. Lake I'm going to come clean with you."

Simon tried to keep calm. "Go on."

"I did meet Kelly Taylor, in my car in a car park. I'd met her previously in the shop – she'd actually flirted with me when I placed the order. She was a nice girl, but cheeky. She let me know that she knew who I was and that I was sending flowers to someone I shouldn't."

"So how did she come to be in your car?"

"She'd phoned me. I'd given her a false phone number when I placed the order because I didn't want anyone to contact me. Anyway she'd recognised me and found my number via the website – the constituency office number is available to anyone. She said she needed to talk to me about the flower order. I said go ahead, what's the problem? She replied there wouldn't be any problem so long as my wife didn't find out what I was up to. I was angry and asked her what she meant by that. She just replied that if she met up with me she'd ensure my little secret remained between us. I didn't really know what the hell to make of it but eventually agreed to see her."

Simon was hanging on his every word. "Go on."

"We met in the car that evening. I'd assumed she'd be coming straight from work but she was all dressed up, make-up on, miniskirt and boots. Looked as if she was off for a night's clubbing. I asked her what she wanted – she was really coming on to me – letting her skirt ride up, showing me what she'd got. I tried not to look and she was making all sorts of suggestive remarks. Eventually she got the message that I wasn't into shop girls and then she changed tack."

"How do you mean?"

"She sat up straight and tugged her skirt down, as if she'd given up on getting me interested and was now moving on to plan B."

"And what was plan B?"

"She told me she was saving up for a new car but it was a real struggle. I knew where she was leading but I didn't say anything. To cut a long story short, she said she knew how wealthy I was and that all she wanted was five grand in cash and then she'd never breathe a word to anyone."

Simon nodded. "So what was your response?"

"I protested, said it was blackmail and that there were severe penalties for that. I said I could go to the police and she'd be in deep trouble."

"And she wasn't fazed by that?"

"Not at all. She laughed at me – said she'd only deny it and that she would make damn sure Louisa knew what I was up to."

"Did you believe her?"

"Bloody right I did. She was so cool, so streetwise, really on the make. I had no doubt whatsoever that she'd stitch me up – she just had so much front."

"So what happened next?"

"I asked her how I could be sure she wouldn't keep coming back for more. She said I'd have to take her word for it but she swore it was a one-off. If I paid up I'd never hear from her again."

"And you believed that?"

"Yes, I did actually. I told her that if she came back for more then I'd figure it could go on forever and I'd come clean and shop her. I told her Louisa would go nuts and I'd be in the doghouse for some time but she wouldn't leave me. I haven't been entirely whiter than white in the past and nor has Louisa, but let's just say we've moved on and we've developed an understanding."

"So you paid up?"

"Yes, I did – a few days later. For five grand it was worth it just to avoid all the hassle. I met her again in the same car park and handed over the ubiquitous brown envelope. Amazing really – she grinned like a little kid with a bag of sweets and actually kissed me as she got out. Incredible!"

There was silence as Simon digested what Halsey had told him. He felt disappointed more than anything, as there was more than a ring of truth about what he'd been told, but – Halsey was a politician. He was used to speaking eloquently and convincingly and he was a past master at talking people into things.

"So you only ever made the one payment to Kelly?"
"Yes."

"But there were umpteen cash payments in the thousands that were deposited into her current account."

"That doesn't surprise me. She was a girl on the make – she had looks and confidence and she wanted the good things in life. I wouldn't be at all surprised if she'd found all sorts of ways to make money. Maybe there were other mug customers like me, maybe she had a sugar daddy and maybe she was working as an escort girl."

"So you are adamant that it was a one-off?"

"Yes I am. I've been totally open and honest with you and if you decide to go the police anyway then so be it. You could ruin my career and cause problems in my marriage, but I swear I never had anything to do with her death. If I have to come clean about everything else then I will. I can handle the disgrace and the hassle, but not any allegation that I hired somebody to murder a scheming little shop girl. I won't get on my knees and beg you, but I am asking you to believe me and then to do whatever you think is right."

Simon nodded dumbly. Halsey might be a clever politician and a good orator but Simon believed him – he just knew that what he'd been told was the truth.

He paused as he opened the car door. "Let me ask you one last question. If you didn't do it, and I know I didn't, then who do you think killed her?"

Halsey paused and looked ahead, out of the windscreen. "Somebody she tried to stitch up, maybe somebody like me. I think she was milking money from somebody and maybe she got too greedy. Maybe she went to Shotley that morning to collect another payment and it all went wrong. I think she targeted men who she knew have got money and a weakness for pretty girls. The florist shop might have given her the perfect opportunity to find her victims. I heard all about the CCTV footage in Sterling Cowell, when she was coming on to you. Maybe she figured you were a potential target too. I think she was always on the lookout."

Halsey started the engine and Simon got out. He watched the Mercedes drive off and he just stood there for a while, thinking about what Halsey had said.

CHAPTER 21

Back in his study, Simon reflected on what had happened. He was no further forward – Halsey wasn't a murderer. He had wasted money on hiring Jeff Clarke and he had wasted his own time following Halsey around. He could have listened to all the advice from everyone around him and saved himself a lot of time, effort and money.

Just as he was wondering whether the whispering would simply die over time, the phone rang.

"Mr. Lake, you think you've got away with it, don't you?"

It was a man, well spoken – he didn't sound like the usual nutters.

"Who is this?"

"Never mind that, Mr. Lake. Who are you? That's the question – are you Simon Lake, a chartered accountant with a nice family and a nice house, or are you a cold-blooded killer who preys on young girls?"

Simon kept quiet.

"You don't have much longer, Mr. Lake – your time is nearly up. You could have come clean, but oh no, you've got to whinge about victimisation and try to get the sympathy vote. Well, I've seen through your little game – you're guilty as hell and very soon the police are going to be visiting you again, but this time you won't be going back home again."

Click – he rang off. Simon dialled 1471 and received the expected 'Caller withheld their number' message.

He sat for a long time, head in hands, sobbing quietly. Even the gin bottle was empty, so he had to resort to brandy. The phone rang again but he ignored it. When the ringing eventually subsided he dialled 1471 again. As he suspected, it was Pippa – he would call her back tomorrow, maybe.

When he awoke the following morning he knew what his next step was. He'd avoided it so far but he was getting desperate. He searched the phone book and found what he was looking for – Taylor D.J. 12 Hayling Street, Ipswich.

He knew where it was – a road of small terraced houses just to the east of the town centre. David Taylor worked as a car mechanic and Simon guessed he wouldn't get home until around six. As far as he knew, Kelly's mum Shelley didn't go out to work. If he phoned first he didn't think they'd agree to see him. No, he had to simply knock on the door once they'd had time to eat their evening meal.

Simon had begun to dread the noise of the phone ringing. Every time he picked up the receiver it was with a feeling of deep foreboding. Either it was an abusive caller, or Peter hassling him to get back to work, or Pippa telling him yet again that he was acting crazy, or maybe it would be DI Whitley telling him to report to the station. He couldn't remember the last time he took a good news call. There was no more good news – it was a microcosm of the ten o'clock news on BBC – death, flood, famine, stock market diving, unemployment soaring, base rate rising and England losing.

By the time he left home that evening he'd had three stiff drinks and he knew he was over the limit. He should walk, it wasn't that far, but he couldn't be bothered. Getting done for drunk driving would simply add to the list. Hayling Street was busy – small houses with no garages and cars parked in every available space. Eventually he squeezed into a little gap with his nearside wheels up on the pavement.

He took a deep breath and rang the doorbell. David Taylor answered the door – he looked as if he had just had a shower and changed after a hard day's work. He had a mouthful of food and was holding a serviette in his hand. They obviously ate later than Simon had expected.

"Mr. Taylor – I'm so sorry. You are obviously eating dinner, let me call back later."

He stared at Simon, weighing him up as he wiped his mouth with the serviette. "I've been half expecting you to come."

"I wondered if you'd recognise me."

"Oh, I recognise you alright. I've read all the papers and watched all the TV coverage ever since the day we lost her."

"Mr. Taylor, I want to find out who killed Kelly, just as much as I'm sure you do. I've been hounded by the police and the press and my life has been made a misery ever since that terrible morning when I found her. I know this is an awkward situation for you, but I'd really like to talk to you and your wife."

He eyed Simon up and down warily, trying to decide what to do. "Okay, come in. We're just finishing our tea."

He showed Simon through into a small kitchen cum dinette. The house was small and simply furnished but spotlessly clean. A woman was clearing plates and sauce bottles from the table. "Shelley, this is Simon Lake – the man who found Kelly's body."

Simon was distressed to see the hostility in her face. "Yes, I know who it is."

She stared at Simon. "What do you want with us?"

"I want to find Kelly's killer, Mrs. Taylor. I know that you and your family can never begin to come to terms with what's happened until the killer is caught, and it's the same for me. Believe me, I am suffering too. I'm disgusted with the police – they don't seem to be getting anywhere."

"There are plenty of people who think it was you."

"Yes, there are, and they'll keep thinking that until the real murderer is found. Right now my life has been ruined, just as yours has. I'm hoping that by finding out all I can then maybe I can give the police the lead they need to get to the bottom of all this."

Her eyes narrowed. "You've been inconvenienced – we've lost a daughter. There's a difference."

Simon nodded. "Yes, when you get it all in perspective I've only been inconvenienced. I feel for you, I really do – but all of us are victims. I've had threatening calls, my house and car have been vandalised and my wife has moved out – but all that is only an inconvenience compared to losing a daughter."

David Taylor pulled out a chair and motioned Simon to sit down with them as his wife finished clearing the dishes away.

When the table was clear Shelley Taylor joined them and put her head in her hands, sobbing quietly. "It's been such a nightmare. Our lovely Kelly – I still can't believe it."

Simon nodded again. "I only met her the once – before I found her that morning – when we were both collecting our cars after they'd been serviced. I didn't even realise that until the CCTV footage came to light. She was just passing the time of day but I remember her being very pleasant. I've got a daughter and so I do think I can imagine just how dreadful it is for you both."

Shelley Taylor stared at him. "We've thought about you a lot – wondering just what happened that morning."

Simon clasped his hands together on the table and looked from one to the other of them. "I wish I'd never gone there. Ever since I was a Ganges boy I've been fascinated by the place. I spent a year there and it shaped my life. I wanted to see what was left – I hoped the remains of my old mess, Blake 7, might still be there. The very last thing I expected to find was a body."

Shelley started to cry and her husband grasped her arm and stroked it. He looked at Simon. "Go on."

"I tried to revive her. I thought there was some warmth still in her and I remembered the first aid training from my Navy days. I did all I could but it was no good, I was too late. I took out my mobile and rang 999, you know the rest."

David Taylor looked impassive. "Obviously we've wondered a lot about you, still do. When the police arrested you we expected them to charge you. We didn't know what to think when they released you. We've heard so little since – the police have been supportive and sympathetic but they don't tell us much. I don't know that they've got any suspects. We knew they were checking on you and on that MP but now it all seems to have gone quiet."

Simon knew the feeling. "Yes, I've been getting so frustrated I've even been doing some checking myself – in fact for a while I hired a private detective to see what he could come up with. We all need closure – you want to see your daughter at rest and I want people to stop hounding me. Only when the person responsible is caught can any of us have a hope of getting on with our lives."

Shelley Taylor looked searchingly into Simon's eyes, trying to weigh him up. "We didn't always approve of the way Kelly lived her life. She never seemed to have boyfriends her own age."

Simon returned her gaze. "Did you get to know any of her boyfriends?"

She shook her head. "No, not at all. Men would sometimes pick her up here but they never came in. I used to wonder if she was ashamed – it's only a council house."

David Taylor was clearly reading Simon's thoughts. "She wasn't a working girl, if that's what you think."

Simon shook his head. "No, I'm sure she wasn't. I had been told she liked the good things in life and that she worked hard to get them – there's nothing wrong in that."

Shelley butted in. "She liked men with money – men who could afford to take her to the best restaurants and for weekends away in posh hotels. None of the lads in her own age group could keep up with her. I used to watch for her coming home late at night – she used to come home in some really posh cars."

Simon raised his head. "Could you ever identify them – did you ever look at their numbers?"

"No, the police kept asking me that. I just know they looked very new and expensive – once I think she even came home in a Rolls Royce."

"Did you tell the police that?"

"Oh yes – they wanted to know the model and colour and number plate and what the man looked like and everything. All I knew was it looked like my idea of a Rolls Royce – I'd no idea about colour or anything, it was dark."

"Did you recognise the make of any other cars she came home in?"

David Taylor intervened. "No, she didn't. I did though – I'm a car mechanic. I've seen her come home in a Mercedes, a Range Rover – and a BMW. I understand that's what you drive?"

Simon nodded. "That's right – but I can assure you Kelly's never been in my car. The police had it for days, the forensic people went all over it."

Taylor shook his head. "I'd bet my life that one of those men took our daughter's life. Whoever killed her knew her – she wasn't out for a Sunday morning stroll and some weirdo just happened across her. Whoever it was had arranged to meet her."

Simon probed further. "It's a strange place and a strange time to meet up with a boyfriend."

Taylor stood up, thrust his hands deep into his pockets and looked out of the little kitchen window. "We've asked ourselves that question over and over again but we never come up with any answers."

"Didn't Kelly confide in you about any of her men friends?"

"No, she was always evasive. I'd ask her about what she'd done the night before and she might tell me which restaurant they'd been to, but nothing more. If I asked her the man's name she'd just give me a first name – I suspected a lot of them were married. She'd get enormous bouquets of flowers delivered here with lovey-dovey messages attached."

"Did she keep the cards?"

"Sometimes, but the police took them all away. They've taken loads of stuff from her bedroom but it doesn't seem to have done them much good."

"So, was she seeing lots of different men for casual dates, do you think?"

"No, they were like men she'd meet and go out with a few times and then she'd move on to someone else. I know what you're thinking, but she wasn't some sort of escort girl. She was just like a typical pretty young girl – it was just that she was choosy. She didn't want some young lad to take her to the pictures or to the pub, Kelly wanted the high life."

Taylor sat down again and clasped his wife's hand. "I sometimes wonder if they'll ever catch the bastard."

Simon stood up. "I'm sure they will, eventually. I don't know what you think about me and I can't really influence you. I just want you to know that when I found your daughter I did all I could. I was in the wrong place at the wrong time but I'm no murderer. I'm a husband and a father and apart from one speeding fine I've never been in trouble with the police in my entire life. I'd like you to believe me, but I know I can't make you believe me. I know that I am totally innocent and one day you'll know that too."

The Taylors just sat there looking down, unspeaking, squeezing each others' hands.

Simon stood up. "I'll bid you goodnight, Mr. and Mrs. Taylor – I'll see myself out."

He drove home slowly, thinking about the world of Kelly Taylor. It seemed strange for a young girl to be quite so materialistic – so fond of men with money. He would have thought she'd have a close circle of boy and girl friends from her schooldays who she'd socialise with regularly and then maybe an occasional date with a sugar-daddy type if she also wanted to sample some of the high life.

The more he thought about it, the more he realised he hadn't learnt anything much from visiting the Taylors. It only really confirmed the fact that Kelly liked rich boyfriends and was a girl with an eye to the main chance. Simon didn't know what his next step should be – he'd pretty much run out of ideas. Just like the police, he suspected.

The next step was defined for him when DI Whitley phoned the following morning.

"Mr. Lake, can you please come down to the station this morning."

It wasn't a question – Whitley was telling him.

"What for? Have you got some new information?"

"No, we just need to go over some things with you again."

"Why? We've been over everything umpteen times. I can't tell you anything more."

"We have to check and double-check everything, Mr. Lake."

Simon sighed. "Okay, I guess I have no choice – but I'll only talk to you with my solicitor present."

It was lucky that John Black was available. He'd had a court appearance cancelled that morning and so agreed to meet Simon at the station.

As soon as they had both arrived Whitley ushered them into the familiar interview room. Simon and John Black sat on one side of the table, with Whitley and a PC on the other. Whitley switched on the tape machine and was straight down to business.

"We've done a huge amount of work, Mr. Lake and I have to tell you that we've eliminated everyone else that has been under any suspicion."

"So what does that mean – you're going to try to pin it on me?"

"We're not trying to pin it on anyone other than the guilty party."

"But you're talking to me again because you haven't a clue who else to talk to?"

It was Whitley's turn to sigh. "The fact is you were at the scene of her death very shortly after she died. There have been no sightings of anyone else and no evidence of anyone else having been there. We have carried out extensive DNA testing of the other suspects and the forensics people haven't come up with anything on them. We have found traces of your DNA all over the body."

"Well, you would do, wouldn't you? How could I attempt resuscitation, the kiss of life, without leaving my DNA?"

"Let me ask you a question Mr. Lake – how could any murderer possibly explain away the fact his DNA was all over a body?"

"I don't know what you mean."

"I mean that the only way would be for the murderer to claim that he found the body and then touched the body for whatever reason."

"So does that mean every person stumbling across a dead body is in danger of being stitched up if the police can't find any other evidence?"

"No, of course not, but it does mean they are sure to be a suspect, possibly the prime suspect."

"You really are clutching at straws. What possible motive would I have for killing her?"

"We don't know, but we do know that Kelly liked men with money. Men who could show her a good time."

"I'm not a wealthy man, I'm simply an accountant."

"You are a partner in a successful firm. You live in a nice big detached house in the best part of town. You drive a BMW. You are exactly the sort of man that Kelly Taylor liked to be with and we have video footage of her talking to you and smiling at you."

"That proves nothing, and you know it. We both collected cars that had been serviced at the same time. You've examined my personal finances and found nothing – because I don't have anything to hide. How could I possibly have been paying her thousands of pounds in cash that wouldn't leave an audit trail?"

"I don't know but I suspect a chartered accountant would know all sorts of smart tricks."

"That is outrageous, Whitley, bloody scandalous. I can't believe you're trying to nail me for this."

"Do you like young girls, Mr. Lake?"

"That's a bloody pointless question. I'm a happily married man with two lovely children and grandchildren – I have a daughter about the same age as Kelly Taylor."

"Is it true that your wife isn't living at your home address at the moment?"

Simon bridled. "She's staying at our daughter Chloe's for a few days. Don't make it into something it isn't."

"When you saw Kelly Taylor at the BMW dealership, what impression did she make on you?"

"Just that she was a pleasant, friendly girl passing the time of day as she waited for her car to come ready."

"What did you think about her physical appearance?"

"That she was a pretty girl, nothing more."

"What aspect of a woman appeals most to you, Mr. Lake?"

"That is a bloody ridiculous hypothetical question that doesn't have anything to do with all this."

"Oh, but it might. Can you please answer the question for me?"

Simon rolled his eyes. "I'm just a typical man of fifty-nine. I'm attracted to a face and a personality more than anything else."

"What about legs and breasts, Mr. Lake – which do you prefer?"

"I strongly object to this. I think this is improper questioning."

John Black interjected. "Yes, I agree. Where do you think you're leading with this line of questioning?"

"It is all relevant to understanding your client's personal likes and dislikes, but I'll withdraw the question if it causes a problem."

Simon was angry. "You're just bloody stumped aren't you? I bet your crime stats are rubbish and your bosses want to know why you've failed to get anywhere with this case despite all the manpower available to you."

Whitley shook his head. "All I can do is the best I can with the leads and the evidence available to me. This is proving to be a very difficult case – the killer covered his tracks really well and had a lot of luck."

Simon actually chuckled. "He got lucky when you were appointed as the investigating officer, you mean."

John Black looked at Simon and shook his head almost imperceptibly. Making fun of a senior policeman when you are a prime suspect isn't a good idea.

Whitley tried to rise above it. "He was lucky that nobody saw him, nobody noticed what cars were parked on the front, nobody was walking their dog at that time. He was also very lucky indeed that you didn't see him as you were at the scene of the crime so very soon after her death."

"Well I didn't see anyone, not a soul. I wish I'd never been there at all but I can't change that now. You can't charge me based on circumstantial evidence."

Whitley leaned back in his chair. "No, we will continue our enquiries. We will find the evidence we need, Mr. Lake – I have absolutely no doubt about that. I'll be in touch. Interview terminated at 1128."

Simon shook his head in disgust, pushed his chair back and stared at the floor.

CHAPTER 22

He walked outside with Black and they stood at the far end of the car park.

"What do you reckon then, John?"

"I think they are absolutely stuck. They don't know what to do next by the look of things."

"And so what do I do?"

"Nothing you can do apart from keep your head down and try to get on with life."

"I can't - life is a bloody mess. I'm avoiding the office because I feel like a freak with everyone staring at me. Pippa thinks I've gone completely loopy and the general public are convinced that I'm a killer. How the hell am I going to get on with life as normal?"

Black shook his head. "I know it's hard, but you've got to keep your head above water. Any day now something could break that gives Whitley and his gang what they need and you'll be off the hook."

"We can dream, but don't hold your breath. I don't rate their chances of ever solving this. I think they'll come under more and more pressure until somebody gets desperate and fabricates some evidence against me."

"That's unlikely – it would be too big a risk. Whitley wouldn't risk his whole career by doing anything like that. He'll get frustrated and plenty of people will say he's incompetent, but he won't stitch you up, he wouldn't dare."

His mood worsened that night when the evening paper came through the door. There on the front page was a picture of him walking into the police station. It had obviously been taken from distance with a zoom lens – the quality wasn't great but it was unmistakably him. The headline was 'Ipswich Accountant Interviewed Again'. If anyone had thought the story would just fizzle out they were clearly wrong. He was right back in the public eye again.

Having lowered the level in the gin bottle considerably he called Pippa. "It's your husband here – remember? The guy in Ipswich who used to live with you …"

"Hello, Simon. Have you been drinking?"

"Can't you think of anything else to ask me?"

"I heard what happened today. It's been on Sky News."

"So you didn't think to call me? To see if I'm okay after being hauled in by the cops again?"

"They said you weren't detained."

"No, that's right – just grilled again and left in absolutely no doubt that Whitley is convinced it was me. All they're doing is looking for one tiny shred of evidence so they can lock me up."

"Well they won't be able to find it, darling, because you're innocent."

"No, but they'll probably fabricate something anyway – Whitley's under pressure to charge somebody and I'm the only suspect he's got."

"Oh darling – are you okay? Are you going in to the office at all?"

"Oh, I'm fine. Sitting here drinking on my own because my so-called friends don't want to know me and my wife's walked out on me."

"Please don't say that – I haven't walked out on you. I just thought it best that I give you some space for a while. Shall I come home?"

"No, don't bother – you're out of the firing line up there. I'll keep an eye out for the police and the vandals while you relax and enjoy yourself."

Pippa tried to remonstrate but he put the phone down.

The next call was from Peter, the following morning.

"Hello, old man. Just phoning to see if you're okay – I read the piece in the paper last night."

"Oh I'm okay – worried, scared, persecuted, lonely but otherwise okay."

"Can I come round and see you, Simon? Never mind all the work stuff, I feel for you, I really do."

"Yeah, why not. Bring the contents of my in-tray if you like. I can't face people in the office but it might do me good to at least try to do something constructive."

"Okay, I will. Are you reading your emails?"

"No, I was – but some of them are pretty scary."

"I'll be round after work – maybe we can just have a chat and a drink?"

"Yeah, sure, see you later."

Peter was as good as his word but Simon was depressed to see that the contents of his in-tray took up three sizable boxes. Simon fixed them both a G&T and Peter updated him on what was happening in the office.

Eventually Peter got down to the nitty gritty. "So when are you coming back?"
Simon avoided his gaze. "It's difficult – I keep hoping something will happen but nothing does."

"You can't stay indoors forever - sooner or later you've got to return to everyday life."

"I know, but just give me a bit longer. I've always had this feeling that it's up to me to find out who did it because I haven't had any confidence in the police right from the beginning."

"How do you think you can solve it when a small army of trained police officers can't?"

"I know, it's bloody mad. Maybe I am going mad."
Peter gripped Simon's arm. "Don't talk like that. Work your way through those boxes and catch up on your emails and then we'll talk about you coming back."

"Okay, I'll give it a try."

"Oh, and while I'm here. Can you give me Charles Dalton's stuff – he's really miffed you've still got it. We really do have to get it back to him."

Simon raised his eyebrows. "I've got to box it all up, it's all over my study right now. I know that I said I'd sort it out but I just haven't got round to it yet. I promise I will in the next few days and then I'll take it over to him and stop him bloody whingeing."

Once Peter had gone Simon put a ready-made lasagne in the microwave and opened a bottle of Chablis. He knew he was drinking too much but what the hell. The bottle was becoming just about the only friend he could lean on.

The next morning he made a half-hearted attempt on the in-tray stuff. Anything that wasn't absolutely essential he binned – only tackling stuff he knew just had to be actioned. All through his working life as an accountant he'd read every issue of Accountancy Age and all the other trade bumf to keep bang up to date. Now he just pushed it all to one side – he wasn't interested in the budget announcements and he didn't even know what new tax-grabbing schemes had spilled from the Chancellor's lips.

By mid-day he was drinking a bottle of lager and browsing through page after page of emails when he heard a key turn in the front door. It was Pippa.

She dropped her case and bag in the hall and climbed the stairs. She smiled, but Simon avoided her outstretched hands.

"Decided to come back, then?"

"Yes, I've been so worried about you - I've come home to look after you."

She looked around the study, taking in the bottles, some spilled crisps, half a packet of biscuits and the piles of paperwork. The floor hadn't seen a Hoover since she left, and the sun shining in through the window highlighted the dust.

Pippa smiled. "I'll get this place cleared up and fix you a proper meal."

"It's okay, I've managed."

"What did the police want with you?"

"Oh, just to go over all the same old ground again. They're stuck and Whitley's trying to figure out how they can pin it on me."

"Oh, I'm sure that's not true. It's just the way they all work, isn't it? Checking and double-checking everything over and over again?"

He sat down and looked at his feet. "I'm at my wit's end – I've just about had enough."

She put her hand on his shoulder. "I think we have to accept that they might never catch whoever did it. There must be lots of unsolved murders on their files. You can't just give up on life. Eventually people will forget; they'll come to realise that if it was you then the police would have charged you. Everyone around here knows that you've been investigated so thoroughly that they'd have been sure to find conclusive evidence if there was anything to find."

He shook his head. "They won't forget, they'll say there's no smoke without fire and people will give me strange looks for the rest of my days. This house is now known to everyone in Ipswich as the place where that suspected murderer lives. I bet every mum and dad for miles around have told their kids to be careful when they come past here and never to talk to that man."

"Oh, come on Simon, it's not that bad – you're becoming really paranoid."

"I'm not, actually. I looked up the dictionary definition of paranoia. It said 'a mental condition characterized by delusions of persecution'. I haven't got delusions of persecution – the graffiti wasn't a delusion, the damage to the car wasn't, and all the hate mail, phone calls and emails aren't. I'm suffering from actual persecution."

Pippa started sobbing and dropped to her knees, head resting against his legs. He put his arm around her shoulders.

"Why us, for God's sake? I thought we had such a good life. The kids have become independent, we're comfortably off, the business was going from strength to strength – and now I feel it's all come to nothing."

Pippa looked up. "Let's go away for a few days, somewhere they don't know us. We need to spend some time together, clear our heads. If you spend some time away from Ipswich then maybe you'll see things in a different light. Let's go walking in Yorkshire."

CHAPTER 23

The Hatton Park Hotel lay in the heart of the Yorkshire moors. Of Georgian design, it overlooked a lake, bordered a golf course and was set in beautiful landscaped grounds. Pippa and Simon checked into their room, showered and changed and were soon sipping G&Ts by an enormous log fire.

Pippa had persuaded him and they'd booked in for three nights. The only person Simon had told was DI Whitley – he didn't want them launching a nationwide manhunt if they decided to check his story yet again.

Simon had even started to feel a bit better on the drive up from Suffolk. As they motored through the hills and dales and marvelled at how green everywhere was, Simon felt some semblance of peace for the first time in months.

They settled into a routine for three days of walking. They slept late and then ate a huge breakfast in the hotel restaurant before pulling on their boots and setting off to walk the moors. Lunch was a pint of Guinness and a sandwich in a handy pub. Dinner was a fine three-course affair with good wine followed by brandy.

The transformation was incredible – they held hands as they walked and back in their room at night they made love for the first time since Simon had found the body. When Simon fell asleep on the second night Pippa snuggled up next to him and cried with relief at getting her old husband back again.

When they checked out and started loading the car, Simon felt mixed emotions. He was as pleased as Pippa that they seemed to have papered over the cracks that had been appearing in their marriage. The change of scenery really had given him a different perspective on life. He realised just what a downward spiral he'd been on, but the elation he felt was tempered by a nagging fear of the future.

Simon had kept his mobile switched off for the whole of the time they'd been away. He'd given Whitley the hotel number, and every evening when they returned from their walk he was relieved to find that there were no messages for him at the reception desk. He still feared that at any moment they would decide to re-arrest him and charge him on some trumped-up evidence.

The optimism of the moors was being replaced by the old gloom as they drove south. Suffolk didn't seem the friendly welcoming place he'd always known before. The house seemed cold and threatening, and he felt that he didn't even want to look at the post or pick up the many phone messages that had accrued while they were away.

They turned the heating back on and Pippa made them both a sandwich while Simon fixed two stiff drinks. They drew the curtains and put their feet up in the lounge.

Pippa broke the silence. "We don't have to live here, you know."

"We do, the business is here."

"You could retire – sell out to Peter and Chris. We could sell this place and move somewhere completely different where nobody knows us – start again. We could afford to buy a really nice little cottage somewhere, play golf, take holidays, live a little."

Simon shook his head. "Do you think running away ever works? Somebody would always stumble across the past, wherever we lived, and then the locals would start whispering and we'd be right back to square one."

Pippa stared into space, shaking her head. "We could change our names."

"Oh no, that would seem like an admission of guilt; and anyway, why the hell should we? That's what makes me so bloody mad – I've done sod all other than to ring 999 when finding a dead body. Sometimes I wish I'd never touched her – just pretended I hadn't seen her and legged it back to the car and driven home."

"No, that wouldn't have been right – and anyway sod's law says that if you had done that you'd probably have been seen by somebody and then you'd have ended up in an even deeper mess."

He got himself another drink while Pippa rang Paul and Chloe for long chats about the trip to Yorkshire. After a night's sleep he felt a little better and even did some work the next day, ploughing through more of the in-tray and even reducing the email backlog to less than three figures. Pippa hoovered and dusted and the house started to look more like the way it always used to.

Late in the afternoon they were in the lounge, enjoying tea and a slice of cake, when suddenly they could hear loud voices outside. Pippa stood up and went to the window.
She gasped, "Oh no, dear God," and closed the curtains.
Simon leapt up from his chair and opened them enough to see out. There were some twenty people outside on the pavement – they looked like young mums and their children on their way home from school. They were holding up a variety of home-made placards. 'Justice for Kelly', 'Keep our children safe' and 'Lock up Kelly's killer' told Simon as much as he wanted to know.

Pippa's face was ashen. "Oh my God, what can we do?"
Simon looked defeated. "Nothing, nothing at all. The police wouldn't help us – free speech, the right to protest and all that stuff."

He peered out of the window again. It was getting worse. He could see a photographer taking pictures – he was standing on the far side of the road so he could get the best shots of all the protesters with the house in the background. A BBC car pulled up and a cameraman started to set up his equipment.

They closed all the curtains and ignored the repeated knocks on the door. Pippa sat in the bedroom in tears while Simon paced the house and repeatedly peered out of gaps in the curtains. It was two hours before the protesters disappeared and another hour after that until the media left.

Simon had phoned the police, but they said that other than getting an officer to pass by and ensure nobody was breaking the law, there was very little they could do.

They watched the late news on BBC, and on the local news at the end of the main bulletin they saw their house and the protesters with their placards. The reporter was matter of fact and said that local mothers had become increasingly concerned that a killer could be in their midst. They interviewed one monosyllabic woman, with a ring through her upper lip, who said she feared for her little girl and had to walk with her to school every day now.

The following morning Simon couldn't even bring himself to leave the house to go to the local shop for the newspapers. Instead he got on the net and looked at the local daily paper's website. Their reproduction of today's front page showed a picture of the house under a headline of 'Ipswich Mums Living in Fear'.

Simon paced the house as Pippa sat slumped in an armchair in the lounge. Neither of them knew what to do – they didn't want to stay in but they didn't want to go out. He didn't even want to check his email in-basket for fear of what might be in there.

Both Paul and Chloe phoned to check they were okay as they'd seen reports of the protest in the paper.

Simon walked into the lounge and put his arm around Pippa's shaking shoulders. "What the hell should we do?"
She shook her head. "I don't know – I just don't know. We can't stay here."
"I'm not going anywhere. It's pointless running away."
Pippa's tears flowed freely. "What a nightmare – it just goes on and on. How long can we stand the stress of all this?"
Simon shrugged his shoulders in defeat. "I think you should go away – go and stay with Paul or Chloe for a while. I'm going to lock myself in and make sure the house stays secure – if we both leave I'm worried that bloody vigilantes will wreck the place."
"Oh Simon, I'm so scared. I don't want to leave you alone but I hate this house now. No matter what happens we need to sell this place – it will never be the same again. We'll have to move."

He knew she was right – their once lovely home felt like a prison. Even if the killer was caught today, life wouldn't ever return to the way it was.

He went to the bathroom and looked in the medicine cabinet. For the first time in his life he wondered what pills you could take when life became too much to handle. There were maybe a dozen paracetamol, a few aspirin, a bottle of indigestion tablets, some tablets for diarrhoea and miscellaneous bits and pieces. It didn't look like the sort of cocktail of drugs that would provide the guarantee of an easy way out. He wondered bleakly what was in the garden shed. Simon shook his head, trying to remove the image from his brain, but with no success.

The doorbell rang again. Simon peered out of the bedroom curtain and was relieved to see Paul's car outside. Simon unlocked and unbolted the front door – Paul had brought an overnight bag.

"Hello, Dad. I've got a couple of days off work so I thought you might want a lodger."

Simon hugged him and then stood back. "It must seem a bit like prison visiting. How the hell did you suddenly get two days off in the middle of the week?"

"An understanding boss – he knows what's going on and he's been really good. He asks me every day if there's any news, and when I told him about your little protest he said I ought to get down here and rally the troops."

Pippa welcomed Paul as if she hadn't seen him for months – kissing him and hugging him. He was a breath of fresh air and immediately took control. He went all round the house drawing back the curtains and even opening windows.

"We're not going to hide, Mum – we're going to stand up for ourselves. We've done nothing wrong and if just one more protester turns up I'm going straight out there to tell them to sod off and pester somebody else."

Pippa shook her head. "We don't want to be confrontational – the police say that would only make things worse."

"Sod the police – what have they done for you and Dad? They've been about as much use as a chocolate teapot and I've had enough, more than enough. It's time to face the world and let them know Dad's innocent and you deserve to be left in peace."

Pippa made them all cheese and ham sandwiches and Paul poured out three beers. They lunched in the dinette and watched the news on TV – mercifully there was nothing more on the protest.

When they'd finished eating, Paul cleared the table and put his jacket on. "Right, you two, it's a nice day so we're going for a walk in the park."

Simon stayed in his chair. "Take your Mum, I'll stay here."

"No you're not - you're coming with us."

Paul fetched Simon's anorak and pulled him up by the arm. "You're both coming with me. We're going to have a good long walk and show the world that we've nothing to feel guilty about and that we're not hiding from anyone."

CHAPTER 24

Christchurch Park was just a five-minute walk away and Paul led them all the way round. The sun was shining, the daffodils were out and little children were feeding the ducks on the pond, despite the notices telling people not to.

When they returned to the house there was a lone reporter outside, looking hopeful. Simon and Pippa walked straight past but Paul challenged him.

"What do you want?"

"I wondered if I could have a word with Mr. Lake."

"What about?"

"His reaction to the protest yesterday."

"No – I want you to leave my Dad alone. I'm sick, tired and fed up over the way he's been hounded. The people who stood outside the house yesterday should be ashamed of themselves. I know they're worried about their kids' safety, but that doesn't give them the right to persecute an innocent man who just happened to be the one who found the girl's body."

The reporter was scribbling furiously. "Can I quote you on that sir?"

Paul thought briefly and then responded firmly. "Yes, actually you bloody well can. My name is Paul Lake and I want the world to know that my Dad has done nothing wrong. There is no evidence against him – if there was one shred of evidence then you can be certain that he'd already have been charged and he'd be locked up. Anyone who says a word against him should be very careful. It's time to hit back – yes, everyone wants justice for Kelly Taylor but I also want justice for my Dad. He's done everything he possibly can to help the police – he's even been spending his own money to try to track the killer down."

The reporter's eyebrows shot up; he couldn't quite believe what he'd heard. "Spending his own money? Could you elaborate on that, Mr. Lake?"

Paul faltered – he hadn't really meant to say that. "It's just that he's concerned the police aren't making much progress and so he had someone else check some things out for him."

"What do you mean sir, a private detective?"

"Something like that – somebody did a bit of surveillance work for him."

The reporter was scribbling faster than ever now. "Surveillance work - who or what were they watching, Mr. Lake?"

Paul just wanted to get away now. "I can't say any more. I just want people to know that my Dad is innocent and he's working with the police to find the killer."

"What is the reaction of the police to your father using a private detective?"

"I can't say any more."

Paul closed the door – Simon and Pippa were already inside.

Simon looked at his son. "I appreciate you standing up for me, but you shouldn't have said all that."

Paul looked down. "Well, you can't just let everyone give you a kicking."

Simon shook his head. "This isn't the right way - it will just put me back on the front page."

Simon was right. On the local news that evening it was the lead story. In the paper the following morning the front page headline was 'Murder Suspect Hits Back'.

They carried an interview with the woman who had organised the protest. She was unrepentant, saying that children should have the right to walk to school without fear. When asked what evidence she had that Simon Lake was a threat to anyone, she replied that there was no smoke without fire. She implied that as they couldn't find anyone else then Simon Lake was a risk to the community.

The story also stated that they had asked Detective Inspector Whitley, who was leading the murder enquiry, what his reaction was to the news that the prime suspect had apparently employed the services of a private detective. Whitley's response was that they didn't condone this and he asked for the local community to have faith in his dedicated team of officers. He said they were leaving no stone unturned in the quest to bring Kelly's killer to justice.

There were two reporters outside on the pavement and Pippa had resorted to drawing all the curtains at the front of the house. Paul was feeling awkward about having stirred up the publicity again but adamant that attack was the best form of defence. Simon was angry with him, telling him to just keep quiet in future. Pippa was simply distraught, wondering what would befall them next.

Simon retreated to his study and forced himself to look at his email in-box. After he had deleted nearly twenty junk emails and scanned some sixty that were work related, there were seven malicious ones.

It amazed him that people would send hate email over the Internet when their sending addresses were plainly visible to him. None of the addresses meant anything to him but he decided to construct a standard response he could use to reply to them all.

The response was a simple statement that he was innocent, had not been charged with any offence, and that anyone making allegations should be aware of the libel laws in the United Kingdom. He sent it to all seven and resolved to send it to each and every future sender of a malicious email. Maybe Paul was right and he should stop hiding himself away and stand up for himself more.

Simon's mood wasn't improved when Peter phoned him.

"I've just had Charles Dalton on the phone again. He is absolutely insisting that he gets all his paperwork back and he's threatening legal action against the firm if he hasn't received it all by the end of tomorrow."

"Okay, okay, I'll do it. I meant to do it before but every bloody time I try to get some work done something happens. You must have seen the latest hassles – it's all a bloody nightmare. Every time we take a step forwards it's quickly followed by several steps back. When you've got protesters outside and you're on the front page of the paper it's hard to motivate yourself to box up a load of sodding accounts paperwork."

"I know and I do sympathise, believe me. If it would help, could I send Jo round to do it?"

"No, it's okay. The stuff is all over the place and I'll just have to do a bit of sorting out before I box it all up. I promise I'll do it tomorrow morning. If you send somebody round to collect it in the afternoon they can deliver it straight to Dalton."

"Okay, old man, sorry to hassle you but we just need to get him off our back."

The next day Paul had to return to work. It was a difficult parting – he'd never seen his Dad so low. He wanted to stay and help but he didn't know what else he could do. He was getting behind schedule with his own work now and he didn't want to test his bosses' patience too far. What really worried him was the impact he could see all this was having on the relationship between his Mum and Dad.

They had been so close all through his life but they were looking like a couple of strangers now. His Dad was showing all the classic signs of paranoia and his Mum seemed nervous about just what to do for the best.

Paul said his goodbyes and did his best to convince them both that everything would work out in the end. From the look in their eyes he knew they didn't share his optimism and he didn't know what else he could say. As he drove off they both waved their goodbyes and then Simon retreated back to his study while Pippa got the Hoover out.

Simon stared unenthusiastically at the piles of paperwork around the room and then started the task of separating all Charles Dalton's stuff, sorting it into piles and getting it all back in to boxes. As he worked through the piles of invoices and statements he separated them in to batches and put elastic bands around them before packing them in to the cardboard document boxes.

He was scornful of the way Charles put every expense he possibly could through the books – and quite a lot that he really shouldn't.

There were numerous receipts for meals, trips to the hairdressers for Janet Dalton, first-class return flights to New York and even one for flowers from him to her on their wedding anniversary. Quite how he thought he would have been able to explain all that to an inspector from the Inland Revenue was beyond Simon.

By the time he was on the eighth box the study was beginning to look a bit tidier and he could see the wood for the trees.

Pippa came in with a mug of coffee. "How are you getting on?"
        "Oh, okay I guess. Getting rid of all Charles Dalton's stuff before he sues me for professional negligence."
She shook her head. "What a bloody shame. All the years you've looked after him. I bet he'd have paid loads more tax with any other accountant."

Simon sighed and gave a rueful smile. "Yeah, well he'll be someone else's problem now. I just can't be bloody bothered any more. There was a time I'd have been mortified at losing the firm its biggest client, but now I just don't give a stuff to be honest."

She put an arm around his shoulder. "One day all this will be behind us, darling. We just have to keep believing."

Pippa returned to her hoovering and Simon to his paperwork. The end was in sight now and he was just sorting through the last bits and pieces and figuring which pile to put what in. There were more petrol receipts, hotel bills, a couple of dry cleaning receipts, several restaurant bills and a copy of an order for more flowers.

It was a duplicate copy of a form similar to those he was given whenever he ordered flowers for Pippa, but the shop name was different. As he went to add it into the pile of other miscellaneous receipts the delivery address caught his eye. Simon blinked, and then read it again – then put his reading glasses on and read it again. He looked out of the window and then back – and read it once more.

'To Miss Kelly Taylor, 12 Hayling Street, Ipswich.' The order was for a twelve red rose bouquet and a box of Belgian chocolates. The card message box was blank, as was the sender's details. The order was dated 12th October and it was for delivery the same day.

He opened the study door and yelled for Pippa. She came running, wondering what the latest emergency could be.

"I want you to read the delivery address on this order form and tell me what it says. Please tell me I'm not bloody seeing things."

Pippa read it – several times. "Bloody hell – bloody hell….and you found this in Dalton's stuff?"

"Yes."

"It's dynamite – absolutely bloody dynamite. Oh, Simon, let's pray to God this is what we think it is."

CHAPTER 25

Simon tried to get his thoughts in order. It wasn't conclusive – it was only an order for flowers. What had Shelley Taylor said when he asked her about the different cars he'd seen Kelly brought home in? One of them looked like a Rolls Royce. Charles drove a Bentley Continental, which looked very much like a Rolls – Simon knew most people probably couldn't tell them apart.

Within five minutes, with the help of Google, he'd found a picture of a car very similar to Charles' on a Bentley website. He printed it off and drove straight to the little house in Hayling Street.

Shelley Taylor was busy cleaning when he arrived. She looked at him warily. "Hello, what brings you back?"

"I'll only take a minute of your time, Mrs. Taylor. I want to show you a picture of a car and I'd like you to tell me if you've ever seen one like it around here."

"Okay, I'll try, but I'm not very good with cars."
She fetched her glasses and Simon handed over the A4-sized picture. The recognition was instant.

"Oh yes, it's like one of the cars Kelly came home in once. I thought it was a Rolls."

"Are you sure?"

"Absolutely certain – you don't see many cars like that stop in this road."

"Thank you very much indeed, Mrs. Taylor, that's all I wanted to know."

"Whose car is it?"

"I'm not certain yet. I think I know who it belongs to but I'm going to hand over what I do know to the police and let them take it up."

"Will it help them to catch him?"

"I hope so, Mrs. Taylor – I very much hope so."

On the drive home he decided he needed more time with Dalton's paperwork. He had told Peter that someone from the office could pick it all up that afternoon. What he needed to do was to go through it all and check for gaps in the audit trail of cash going through the business. If Dalton was the one supplying the sums of cash Kelly paid in to her account then he needed to find out where it came from.

Simon knew that some of Dalton's tenants still paid their rent in cash. While many had set up direct debits or paid online via BACS, there were still people who liked dealing in cash. Some shopkeepers with large cash takings hated paying bank charges for simply depositing their hard-earned money and so they used cash to pay many of their bills.

Simon had experienced problems with Dalton in the past, where he had simply used some of the business cash for personal expenditure. As an accountant Simon knew this was exactly the sort of thing an Inland Revenue inspection would home in on. He had frequently told Dalton that the annual accounts simply had to balance. All income had to be accounted for, whether it was cash, cheque, electronic, whatever.

In the past Dalton had simply claimed to have forgotten about the odd few hundred pounds here and there that had gone into his wallet rather than into the business. If he was Kelly's benefactor then there would probably be thousands of pounds of missing cash from somewhere in the last year's accounts. Simon needed to find the discrepancies and he needed to find them fast.

As he gazed out of the study window he actually smiled. No wonder Dalton was in such a panic to get his paperwork back. He would know that the flower order form was with the prime suspect and in all probability he knew that the evidence of unaccounted cash was too.

It was likely that Dalton had done something clever to hide the cash. He would know that Simon couldn't balance the accounts if he simply siphoned off bundles of cash. Somehow he would have covered himself – maybe by having a cash tenant whose records simply didn't go through the books. This could be hard to find but Simon knew he had to try.

He called Peter at the office and lied. He said he had started work on Dalton's paperwork but had been sidetracked - he was required to spend some more time down at the police station. He told Peter to let Dalton know that he was very sorry but that he would have all his stuff back by Monday at the very latest. This gave Simon all weekend to search through it.

When Pippa returned from a trip to the supermarket she couldn't wait to find out the latest.

"What did Shelley Taylor say?"

"That the car she'd once seen Kelly come home in definitely looked just like the one in the picture."

Pippa eyes were out on stalks. "So what do we do now?"

"We work - we've got the weekend to find out if Dalton was siphoning off cash from the business to feather young Kelly's nest."

"Can I help?"

"Yes, you certainly can. It will mean lots of searching, spreadsheet work, checking payments from tenants and matching payments in to the bank accounts. It'll be a bit like searching for a needle in a haystack, but I think that somewhere in here is the missing piece of the jigsaw. Don't expect to get much sleep this weekend."

"I'll do whatever you want – we can sleep next week."

Over the next three days and nights they worked like never before. Pippa was both nervous and excited – it was as if the thrill of the hunt had reunited them, made them a team again.

She searched, collated and checked figures as instructed while Simon beavered away on the computer. He was using his accounting system and multiple Excel spreadsheets. Occasionally Pippa would break off to fetch them fresh mugs of coffee and sandwiches.

They ignored the phone and knocks at the door. As they worked through each tenant's records they found evidence of payments made and where the payments went. By Sunday afternoon they were both feeling tired and disappointed that so far they hadn't found the missing cash. By that evening they had been through the lot, still without success. Simon had found all sorts of little discrepancies – an unaccounted fifty pounds here and a hundred there – but nothing substantial.

The initial excitement had worn off. Tiredness was really kicking in – Pippa had snatched about three hours' sleep the night before but Simon had kept going all the way through the night. He had only left the study to visit the bathroom when he had to, but now he was feeling the strain.

Late that evening he let out a huge sigh. "Well that's it – we've been through the lot now. Whatever he was getting up to with Kelly, I don't think we have any proof that he was her sugar daddy."

Pippa felt his dejection. "You could still go to the police with the flower order. That would be enough for them to start checking him out."

Simon shook his head. "No, we need more than that. It seems that Kelly had lots of wealthy boyfriends. We need to find the one she was making serious money from."

Pippa gazed out of the window. "Are you hungry?"

"Yes, I am. It's ages since we last had a sandwich."

"What do you fancy?"

"What I really fancy is fish and chips, but I don't suppose anyone is open on a Sunday night."

Pippa looked thoughtful – then she stared at Simon, open-mouthed. "What about Tony's on Colchester Road?"

"No – I know for a fact he's closed all day Sunday."

"That's not what I mean."

Simon was puzzled. "Come again?"

"Tony's on Colchester Road. I thought Dalton owned that place?"

It was the eureka moment. Simon hugged her and kissed her. "Brilliant, absolutely bloody brilliant. He does, and it's not on the list of tenants – there's nothing in all this stuff that has any connection with the shop whatsoever."

"You're sure it's one of his?"

"Definitely – if he'd sold it I'd know about it – I would have handled the capital gains tax. It used to be a cycle shop and then it was empty for a while. He's got so many properties I just forgot all about it. No – it's still Dalton's and there isn't one penny of rent from that place shown in any of this stuff. It's a big shop, too, it used to be two shops and then he had it knocked in to one. It had really good rent potential as it's in a really prime position – that is such a busy road and it has good parking at the front."

Pippa digested all this for a while. She had spent quite a bit of time helping Simon with accounts stuff over the years and so had a rudimentary understanding of how small businesses worked.

Eventually she looked up. "But how would all this make any sense for Tony? If he's not putting his rent payments through the books then it is just artificially inflating his net profit and he'll be paying more tax."

Simon smiled. "You're right, but Dalton can afford to give him a really good deal. It will increase Tony's profits and his tax liability but it will lower Dalton's declared income and so he'll pay less corporation tax. He's making such huge profits that he's paying corporation tax at thirty per cent. He can easily afford to give Tony a really hefty discount on his rent if he pays cash."

Pippa thought some more. "But wouldn't all this come to light if Tony had a tax inspection?"

"No – the Inland Revenue doesn't give a stuff if somebody under-declares their outgoings. It simply means they pay more tax. The inspectors are only interested in people who are working a con and either understating their income or overstating their outgoings. So long as they don't think the declared profit is too small they don't really give a damn."

"What about the VAT angle?"

"No problem – rent isn't VATable."

Pippa stood up and walked around the room deep in thought. "Given that Dalton's got so much money anyway, I don't understand why on earth he would go to all this bother – this would be just small change to him."

"It's virtually untraceable money, that's the big attraction. It's probably at least twenty grand a year in cash that could be used for dubious purposes, without anybody finding out. Almost all of his normal expenditure leaves an audit trail but this doesn't."

"So what do we do next?"

"First thing tomorrow morning I'm going to make a few enquiries – just to make absolutely sure Dalton still owns the freehold and our suspicions are correct."

Pippa smiled. "This is worth a drink."

It was indeed – he fixed two large G&Ts and when they'd downed them he fixed two more. They still didn't sleep well that night, though. Simon was itching for the time to pass so that he could contact people the following morning and move things on. Pippa was excited and jumpy – they seemed to be on to something but she knew they were still a long way from clearing her husband's name.

The morning dawned bright and clear and Simon had showered and shaved and was busy working in the study by seven. It seemed that the Land Registry people didn't start work until nine, but he was ringing their number at one minute past. It took just over an hour to establish that the shop freehold was indeed registered to a Mr. Charles Dalton.

The next call was to Tony Cardino at Tony's fish and chip shop. As Simon had hoped, he wasn't in, but the phone was answered by Sheila, one of his staff.

"Hello there, I was trying to contact Tony's accountant. He isn't there by any chance, is he?"

"Mr. Walker? No, I'm sorry, he only usually pops in about once a month."

"Okay, no problem, thanks."

Simon knew Joe Walker; he looked after the books of numerous small businesses around the Ipswich area. He found his number and dialled. "Hello Joe, it's Simon Lake here."

"Hello Simon, haven't heard from you for ages. How are you?"

"Oh, I'm okay apart from all the hassle I've had since finding a dead body."

"Yes, I've read all about it. It all seems to have gone quiet again."

"It has. I live in hope that they'll catch him one day but I'm not holding my breath."

"So, what can I do for you?"

"We've got a client who has a fish and chip shop and it's coming up for a rent review. It's the usual situation, with the landlord proposing a massive increase, and so I'm ringing around trying to find out what the going rate is for similar premises around Ipswich."

"Okay, I understand, how can I help?"

"Well, this shop is a similar size to Tony's on Colchester Road and it's in a prime position, just like his place is. I know you do his accounts and so I'm hoping you can tell me what he's paying in rent."

"Sorry Simon, I'd help if I could, but Tony holds the freehold and so rent isn't an issue."

"Oh I see, lucky Tony."

"Yes, I was surprised he owned the place. It's a big shop and there's a nice three-bedroom flat above it that is part of the premises – that's where Tony lives."

"I see – did he buy the freehold recently?"

"No, he's certainly had it ever since I've been doing his accounts. I don't know quite how long but it must be several years at least."

"Okay Joe, no problem – thanks anyway."

Pippa was standing by the door. "So what was the answer?"

"As expected – his accountant thinks Tony owns the freehold and no rent goes through the books. He also told me Tony lives in a nice big flat over the shop, so the real rent will be even higher than we thought – probably the best part of thirty grand to cover the shop and the flat."

Pippa smiled ruefully. "Thirty grand of untraceable readies for Charles Dalton to fund extra-curricular activities with?"

"That's about the size of it."

"So what now?"

"I had thought I'd call Whitley and arrange to go and see him, but I might leave it a little while longer. The combination of the flower order, the car sighting and the missing money should give him plenty to work on. First, though, I'm going to let Dalton have all his paperwork back, all apart from the flower order form, and then we can see what the reaction is."

Jo duly called at the house and Simon and Pippa helped her to load all the boxes into her car. She was delivering them straight to Dalton at his office.

He only had to wait until first thing the following morning before Peter rang. "Hello, Simon old man – look, I've had a call from Charles Dalton. He's grateful for finally getting his paperwork back but he says it's not all there – there must be something missing."

Simon smiled to himself. "He was quick to find that out – he only got it mid-afternoon yesterday and there's an awful lot of stuff to sort through."

"Yes, I know, but he's adamant it's not complete and he wants the rest."

"Sorry, Peter, but it's everything I had. Tell him that if he likes to let me know what he thinks is missing then I'll double check."

Simon would have bet his house on Dalton not coming back to him - and he didn't.

CHAPTER 26

Whitley sounded almost resigned and bored on the phone when Simon insisted on seeing him. Only when Simon told him that he had new and very revealing information did he show any interest at all.

When Simon handed him the flower order form, Whitley sat bolt upright. Then he explained about Shelley Taylor's sighting of a car just like Dalton's bringing Kelly home. When he followed that up by explaining he'd found a hole in Dalton's accounts where Kelly's cash could have come from, Whitley looked totally gobsmacked.

"You have been busy, Mr. Lake, and although your methods might not be conventional I have to admit I'm impressed."

"Well, now I want you to impress me. I want you to make the most of a golden opportunity."

Whitley nodded. "Okay, I have to admit the flower order certainly looks very interesting. There's more than one car in the Ipswich area that looks like a Roller, though, and the cash discrepancy in Dalton's accounts could simply be a fairly minor case of fiddling the books."

"Don't soft-pedal on this, Whitley – it's dynamite and you know it."

"I promise you we'll follow this up right away, Mr. Lake – I can assure you that if this gives us the lead we've been hoping for then nobody will be more pleased than me."

As soon as he was back home again, Simon called John Black to put him in the picture. He was impressed with the news but disappointed that he hadn't been at the police station to see Whitley's face.

Simon and Pippa were like the proverbial cats on a hot tin roof for the rest of the day. They couldn't concentrate on anything as they paced the house watching the TV news channels, listening to local radio and surfing for news on the net. Infuriatingly, just when they wanted the phone to ring, it didn't.

They had to wait until the early evening regional TV news until there was a development. The anchorman interrupted a piece about how new EU farm subsidies could impact local farmers.

"We have breaking news that a man has been arrested in connection with the murder of Kelly Taylor. A police briefing has just announced that Charles Dalton, aged fifty-three, was arrested at 3pm this afternoon at his office in Ipswich and taken to an undisclosed police station for questioning. Mr. Dalton is understood to be a well-known property magnate who owns a large portfolio of both residential and commercial property in the Ipswich area. The police declined to take any questions at the press briefing and said they would be making a further announcement in due course."

Within seconds the phone started ringing, and Simon then took a series of calls throughout the rest of the evening and into the early hours of the following morning.

He gave a full explanation of what had been going on to Paul, Chloe and Peter, brief details to numerous other friends and work colleagues, and very little to the many reporters who were suddenly back on the case. The only exception was John Greaves from the Mail, who had proven his reliability when Simon had decided to go public before.

Simon was still urging caution – telling everyone that it was only another arrest and reminding them that he had been arrested himself and then released without charge. John Black said it was a racing certainty that the police would be carrying out DNA tests on Dalton and much would depend on the results of those tests.

By the following morning Dalton's arrest was being widely reported by all of the media. There were various mentions that the arrest would take the pressure off Ipswich accountant Simon Lake.

John Greaves had written the most detailed account in the Mail – he mentioned that should Charles Dalton prove to be guilty then a lot of people were going to owe Simon Lake a full apology.

It was another day of pacing the house, watching the news on TV and listening to the news on the radio at the same time. Simon felt the knots in his stomach as he half expected an announcement at any moment that Charles Dalton had been released without charge.

The media had moved their attention to Dalton's palatial home, and every TV news bulletin was showing interviews with their reporters with the locked gates in the background. ITN and Sky both showed footage of Janet Dalton drawing up in her silver Lexus 4×4. As she waited impatiently for the electronic gates to open, the cameras clearly captured the face of a very worried-looking lady in sunglasses. You could feel her relief when the gates opened enough for her to sweep through. A gardener struggled to keep back the media scrum as the gates closed behind her.

Simon tried to picture Dalton sitting in the interview room with Whitley, going through what he had experienced himself. He could only hope that Dalton wasn't coming up with a clever cast-iron alibi that would somehow prove his innocence. There had been so many setbacks and disappointments ever since that awful day when he found Kelly's body that nothing would surprise him any more.

He found sleep hard to come by that night. When he eventually dropped off, it was only to enter a dream where Dalton was looking through the study window, laughing at him and taunting him, as the police hammered on the front door and demanded access.

He was both listening to the radio and watching the TV when the six o'clock news bulletins came on. There was no news other than statements that there were no further developments and the police had to either charge Dalton or apply for an extension to keep him under arrest.

Pippa was in a quandary, as she had promised Chloe that she would travel to London that day so that she could babysit the two girls that night. Jason's company was putting on a lavish dinner dance at the Inn on the Park and Chloe had asked her Mum months ago if she would come and stay. Jason was being presented with a special award and Pippa didn't want to let them down. Simon eventually talked her into going and drove her to the station to catch the 1030 train to Liverpool Street. She made him promise to keep his mobile switched on and to call her just as soon as there was any news.

Simon had only been back at home for ten minutes when John Black called him. "Simon, I've got big news for you."

"Go ahead."

"Are you on your own?"

"Yes, Pippa's gone to London. Get on with it, for Christ's sake."

"I've been down at the station this morning – trying to stop a drunken client talk himself in to even more trouble."

"Get on with it, John."

"There was loads of activity; the place was like a bloody hornet's nest and it wasn't hard to find out why."

"Is there any chance you'll come to the bloody point eventually?"

"I'm sorry. The news is – and this is absolutely confidential at this stage – Dalton has been charged with murder."

Simon felt numb, unable to speak.

"Evidently he's made a full confession. He didn't even wait for the results of the DNA tests to come back. Once they explained exactly what they were testing for and how the DNA process works, he just held his hands up – he knew there was no possible way out."

Simon gazed out of the study window – thinking it must be a good spring for the birds as they still hadn't eaten all of the nuts Pippa had put out for them.

"Simon, are you still there? Say something, man."

"It's very good news, John – Kelly's mum and dad will be very relieved."

"Is that it? How about you?"

"I'm okay. Do you know any more?"

"Yes, but I can't tell you now. What I can tell you is that you are completely in the clear. The nightmare is finally over. Look, I'm going to come straight over and I'll explain more then. The police have announced a press briefing for twelve o'clock – we can watch it together on your TV. Right now, though, you can't tell anyone anything more, not without dropping me right in it. I know far more than I should because through sheer luck I just happened to be in exactly the right place at exactly the right time."

Simon walked into the back garden – both the magnolia and the camellia were in full bloom and the grass really needing cutting. The bird feeder was half empty so he removed the top of it and poured in the remaining contents of a packet of sunflower seeds. He picked up the watering can and filled both of the bird-baths.

He noticed that Pippa had set some new plants in the rockery; he wondered what they were. He sat on a chair on the patio and stared into space until John Black walked round the side of the house.

"Oh there you are - I've been ringing your doorbell for the last five minutes."

"Sorry, John. Come in – I'll make some coffee."

CHAPTER 27

They sat in the kitchen and watched the press briefing on TV. Whitley looked as if he'd had no sleep for ages, and Simon guessed that this was probably because he hadn't. The announcement was brief and to the point – it didn't add anything to what Simon already knew.

John Black had a wide smile on his face. Simon thought he looked like a little lad who had just had his complete wish list for Christmas okayed.

"Who'd have thought it, eh, Simon? Mr. bloody Charles Dalton, pillar of the community, entrepreneur, old Etonian, rich bastard, Rotarian and murderer."

"How much do you know?"

"Plenty, I got very lucky."

"How come?"

"My mobile's battery was very low and so one of the PCs let me use a phone on a desk in the corner of their office. Anyway, the PC got called away and I was left in there on my own. It was open-plan, but with shoulder-height partitions around the desks. The desk was covered with paperwork and so I put my briefcase on the floor and started rooting around in it to find the number I needed.

I heard somebody come in, but they didn't see me as I was on my knees busily searching through my case. Then somebody else came in to the room and I heard them let out a whoop – like their football team had just scored a last minute winner.

I heard a voice ask what he was so pleased about. He replied that Charles Dalton had just made a full confession to the murder of Kelly Taylor and he proceeded to give his colleague chapter and verse on it. I stayed out of sight, on my knees – I couldn't avoid hearing every word he said."

Simon nodded. "So what exactly did he say?"

"That Dalton had been seeing Kelly for a while. She first eyed him up when he was having dinner with Janet at that posh French restaurant in the docks. She was there with someone else, but when Janet went to the Ladies she gave him a smile to get him interested. He only slipped her a business card when he was on his way out – bloody cool as a cucumber.

So she phones him the next day, he takes her out for a couple of meals – well away from Ipswich, of course – and then after a while they started using a room at a Travelodge for a couple of hours. Just imagine that, Simon – Charlie bloody Dalton in a Travelodge! Who'd have believed it?"

Simon washed the coffee mugs up.

"Anyway, before long Kelly's saying she's short of money and telling him she was saving up for a new car. Dalton slips her the odd hundred quid here and there, but of course that's not enough for Kelly. She starts making noises about how dreadful it would be if Janet was ever to find out about their sordid little affair. So the prezzies start getting a bit bigger and young Kelly's looking in the showroom window at the BMW dealership."

Simon nodded, and started to unload the dishwasher. John watched him, shaking his head. "So anyway, the situation develops further – Kelly's wearing her sauciest undies, spending afternoons with him, on her back, and the Travelodge's occupancy rate is improving. By now Kelly's letting him know that she thinks the three-digit gifts are a bit mean, so he's handing over a thousand a time.

Things come to a head one night when Charlie-boy's having a shower after a particularly raunchy session. Kelly says she doesn't want to just be his secret little bit on the side – she wants some recognition. She threatens to talk to Janet and Charlie panics, forking out more money."

Simon was looking in the kitchen cupboards, wondering what to eat for dinner that night.

"Bloody hell, Simon, I'm not boring you, am I?"

"Sorry, no – carry on."

"Well, so it goes on, with Kelly playing him like a bloody fish. Amazing, really – a little florist and a mega-rich property baron, but it was obvious who had the trump cards. She gets more and more pushy, and it becomes obvious that she'll stop at nothing. After a while Charles can see his marriage collapsing and his reputation being ruined, so he decides he'll have to get rid of her – he's never been one for half measures."

Simon put some potatoes in the sink, ran some water and started peeling them. "So how did he get her to come to Shotley on a cold Sunday morning?"

"Kelly had been pushing ever harder – she demanded ten grand or else she was going straight to Janet. Charles said the only time he could get it to her was on that Sunday morning. He told her he wanted them to stop seeing each other but he'd pay her what she wanted, and he'd add a final bonus to buy her silence.

Well, evidently Charles didn't believe she'd ever stop screwing money out of him, so he figured he had to get rid of her. He said he was going sailing for the day with a friend who had a boat at the marina there. If Kelly drove out there he'd see her one last time and hand over the cash, but he told her they'd have to be very careful not to be seen together. He said the old Ganges site would be best and he told her where to park and how to find the gap in the fence. She was so eager to get the cash she didn't take any precautions, and once Charles was absolutely certain that she'd come there alone he knew he had to seize the opportunity."

"So he strangled her?"

"Yes – he's a fit strong guy. All that time he spends in the gym meant Kelly hadn't got a chance. He'd actually been doing research to find out just how and where to best apply the pressure – amazing what you can learn on the bloody Internet these days."

"Thanks a lot, you must let me have your bill."

"Sod the bill – for God's sake, Simon, you should be dancing on the roof."

Simon smiled. "Yes, it's very good news, thank you."

John shook his head in amazement. "Must be the shock of it all, I guess – it'll take time to sink in. Anyway, I really must go. Look after yourself, Simon, and don't say anything to the press – you ought to take Pippa out for a big celebration dinner."

"Yes, I suppose so. Bye, John."

He felt sure there would be some parsnips somewhere. Pippa knew how much he liked parsnips – she would surely have left him some. Right on cue the phone rang. "Simon, it's me – Pippa. Have you seen the news?"

"Yes, I have – sorry, I was going to phone you. John Black's just been here giving me all the details."

"It's fantastic, darling – Chloe and I have been laughing and crying at the same time. The release of emotion is just incredible – you must be feeling so relieved."

"Yes, darling, it's good."

"Good? Is that all you can think of to say?"

"No – well, I can't find any parsnips. Where are they?"

"Bloody hell, darling – all the excitement must have scrambled your brain. You'll find some in the cupboard to the left of the sink. But why bother with bloody parsnips – crack open the champagne, for goodness sake!"

"Yes, I'll probably have a drink. When are you coming home?"

"I'd like to come tonight, but I've told Chloe and Jason they must go to their do. I'll get the train back in the morning – I'll be home by lunchtime."

"Okay darling. Oh – and Pippa ..."

"Yes?"

"I do love you. I always have. I want you to know that – it's important."

She laughed. "Yes, of course you do, darling – and I love you too."

Simon got the mower out of the shed. It would be the first time this year that he had cut the grass and it took a while to get the mower started. He wondered if he should have changed the oil during the winter.

Every time the grass box was full, he emptied it into the bin and then sat down on a bench for a while and looked around the garden, wondering what other jobs needed doing. When he eventually went back into the house the phone was ringing.

"Hi Dad, it's Paul. I've been trying to get through to you for ages. Mum gave me the news. Where on earth have you been?"

"Oh hello, sorry – I've been cutting the grass."

"Cutting the grass? Bloody hell Dad, you're a cool customer – you should be down the pub celebrating. I'm just so pleased for you – all those people who doubted you must be feeling pretty bloody silly now."

"Yes, I suppose so."

"You don't sound very upbeat, Dad – I thought you'd be over the moon."

"Well I want to cook a meal tonight but your Mum seems to have hidden the parsnips."

"Is that really important at a time like this?"

"I like parsnips."

"Well, anyway, I'll get down to see you very soon and then we'll all celebrate in style. Take care of yourself, Dad. I love you."

Paul sat for a while, as if in a trance, just staring at the phone. He jumped as it rang again – it was his mum.

"Hi Paul – I'm at Chloe's. Jason has been able to get the day off work tomorrow and they're going to drive me home in the morning. A friend of Chloe's is going to look after the girls for the day. We're planning a bit of a surprise party for your Dad. Can you get down for it?"

"Sure I can – I wouldn't miss it for the world. I'll throw a sickie if I have to. Shall I see you at the house?"

"No, let's meet up at the Sainsbury's on the way into Ipswich at around twelve. We're stopping there to buy some champers, food and balloons and stuff. We're going to give him a big surprise – he really needs a lift after all that's happened to him."

"Yeah he does, but do you think balloons and stuff are appropriate? How did he sound when you spoke to him on the phone?"

"Well, a bit weird, actually – not quite with it. I think it's just the shock of everything – he's been so worried for so long and now that it's all over it's hard for him to take it all in. He'll be all right though – once he's had a good night's sleep and we all turn up tomorrow, he'll be fine."

"I'm not so sure, Mum – this could take a bit of time. I guess it's a bit like post-traumatic stress. I'm not at all sure that he's really taken it all in yet. He was banging on about bloody parsnips."

Pippa laughed. "Don't worry – we'll look after him. It's going to be great tomorrow, the whole family back together again for a big celebration – I can't wait."

Simon tidied up the flower-beds and put all the rubbish into the bins – making sure to put the garden rubbish in the brown bin and the newspapers in the blue bin. He collected up all the empty bottles and put them in carrier bags, ready to go to the bottle bank at the supermarket. He washed his hands and headed back to his study. He tidied up all his paperwork and wrote out cheques to pay the phone bill and the water rates – he put them in envelopes and left them by the phone in the hall, ready for posting.

He found the parsnips in the end and cooked himself a dinner of roast beef, roast potatoes and three veg. He even made himself a Yorkshire pudding. He sat in the dinette in silence and drank most of a bottle of Shiraz with the meal. The phone rang several times and so he took the receiver off the hook. Someone knocked at the door but he just ignored it. He was in bed by ten and he slept like a baby.

The rest of the family met as planned at Sainsbury's – there were hugs, kisses and high fives as they greeted each other as if they hadn't been together for years. Paul bought three bottles of Moët et Chandon and Jason found balloons, party poppers and streamers. Pippa and Chloe bought the food – smoked salmon for the starter, the very best rib steak they could find for main course, and even Simon's favourite dessert – bread and butter pudding.

With everything loaded into the cars they drove in convoy to the house and, finding the front gates open, they both pulled in and parked in the driveway.

Pippa was like a little girl – she was just so excited. She beamed at Paul. "I hope your Dad is in."
        "I guess he must be, with the gates open."
Pippa cocked her head on one side. "I can hear a car engine."
Paul listened – she was right. "I'll check it out, Mum."
Pippa made to follow him but he stopped her. "No, Mum, you unload the car and I'll find Dad."

He walked towards the garage and the sound got louder. The up-and-over door was closed, but there was a side window in the garage wall. Paul cupped his hand against the glass to provide a shield against the sun. He peered through. The length of hosepipe leading from the exhaust pipe in through the driver's window confirmed his worst fears.

Heart pounding, stomach churning, he pulled up the garage door and choked as the fumes hit him. He wrenched open the car door and switched off the engine. His Dad was slumped forwards over the steering wheel. Handkerchief clamped over his mouth, Paul felt in vain for a pulse. He knew there would be no surprise party.